FOSTER CHILD

Also by Marion Dane Bauer

SHELTER FROM THE WIND

FOSTER CHILD

MARION DANE BAUER

A CLARION BOOK

THE SEABURY PRESS · NEW YORK

The Seabury Press, 815 Second Avenue, New York, New York 10017

Printed in the United States of America

Library of Congress Cataloging in Publication Data

Bauer, Marion Dane.   Foster child.
"A Clarion book."
Summary: When her great-grandmother is placed in a nursing home, a twelve-year-old is sent to a foster home where the fanatically religious father presses his attentions on her.
[1. Foster home care—Fiction] I. Title.
PZ7.B3262Fo   [Fic]   76-54291   ISBN 0-8164-3190-6

X
C.1

*This book is dedicated to
Maia Wojciechowska,
who believed in the first* FOSTER CHILD *and in me,
and to
Madeleine L'Engle,
who has sustained me with caring.*

FOSTER CHILD

1

"YOU'LL like the Becks, Lorraine." Miss Kistner, the social worker, lifted her chin to peer over the hood of her old blue Ford. She maneuvered it off the highway and onto a dirt road that separated two winter-bare fields. "They've been keeping foster children for us for ten years now, and they're lovely people. Besides, it's time you were part of a family."

"Gram is my family," Renny said, without turning to look at Miss Kistner.

"But my dear, your great-grandmother is ill, and she's seventy-nine years old. It's time she had a rest. The hospital is taking good care of her."

"I could have taken care of her."

Miss Kistner's voice was gentle, wheedling. "You are only a little girl. You need taking care of yourself."

"I'm twelve years old." Renny turned to look at Miss Kistner for the first time since they had left Great-Aunt Florence's apartment in River Bluffs. "And I've been taking care of Gram for a long time. I brush her hair and make her tea. I even do lots of the housework. We take care of one another. We always have. There was no need to take her to the hospital. Great-Aunt Florence had no right to send me away."

"Your great-aunt was only thinking of you, Lorraine. She wanted what was best for you." Miss Kistner turned into a bare yard at the end of the lane and stopped the car.

"Great-Aunt Florence never thought of anybody but herself in her whole life." Renny felt herself flush as she spoke. Gram would be ashamed to hear her. Gram had never said her daughter, Florence, was selfish. Gram never said anything bad about anybody. But Florence had moved out, lived by herself. Renny never meant to leave Gram, not ever. If Great-Aunt Florence hadn't called the ambulance. . . .

"Now, Lorraine . . . ," Miss Kistner reached over to touch Renny's hand, and Renny drew back. Miss Kistner let her hand drop onto the car seat between them. The evening sun slanting through the car window turned the social worker's hair into a frizzy gray halo. "Missouri law doesn't allow twelve-year-olds to live by themselves, not even in their great-grandmother's house, so Miss Morrison had no choice. She would have kept you herself, but she knew you needed other children, parents."

"I wouldn't want to stay with her anyway." Renny was watching some chickens pecking at the frozen ground. She couldn't imagine what they were finding to eat. She avoided looking at the house, its paint peeling. "Is it a farm?" she asked.

Miss Kistner gathered her large handbag. "No," she

answered cheerfully, "the fields don't belong to the Becks, just the house. Mr. Beck bought this place when they first began to take children for us because he wanted a healthy environment for them. That is how dedicated he is—they are. They even left their own home to come here."

Like me, Renny thought, but this time she didn't speak.

When they got out of the car, a bitter February wind drove them toward the front door, which was opened by a skinny little girl with red hair straggling around her face. She stared, then turned and scurried away down the dark hall. "Mom Beck," she could be heard calling in the distance, "Miss Kistner is here with a new girl." A paper airplane whooshed down the stairway and hit the screen, still closed between them and the house. A boy in jeans and a dirty yellow shirt roared up to the door, snatched the plane, gazed at them a moment, and then flung himself back down the hall, making sound effects for an entire air force.

"Ah, David?" Miss Kistner said, looking up from the small notebook she had begun leafing through when the first face had appeared at the door; but David, if it was David, had disappeared. Renny stepped backward a step and felt the edge of the porch sag with her weight. She moved forward again, keeping Miss Kistner between herself and the doorway. A fat woman was making her way down the hall, pushing brownish gray hair out of her eyes, wiping her hands on a soiled apron. She wore a cotton dress with large poppies all over it. Renny could see a gaping tear under one arm—right through the middle of a poppy. "Miss Kistner, how are you? Get yourselves in here. And this must be our new little girl. How're you? Let's see, Miss Kistner told me your name's Lorrene? We're happy yer here, Lorrene. You'll find us jist one big, happy family here. Always room for one more. Jist takes a bit more water in the soup."

The woman winked at Miss Kistner, as if the whole thing were some kind of private joke between them, but she didn't pause for a breath. "Come in. Come in. I'll have to tell that Karen about running off and leaving you standing here. Kids don't think. All so busy with theirselves. Never think of anyone else. Now, Lorrene, let me show you where to hang your coat. Might as well start off right. No one gets waited on around here, except maybe we trot for Mr. Beck a little. Always good to keep a man happy, you know. They work better that way." Again the wink in Miss Kistner's direction as Renny felt herself propelled down the hallway, past the stairs, toward a jumble of overshoes and a rack hung with an assortment of coats. "Now, Lorrene. . . ."

"Her name's Lorraine, Mrs. Beck. Lorraine, this is your foster mother, Mrs. Beck."

"Oh, 'scuse me. Lorraine. You'll have to help me with that every now and then, child. I'm awful with names. You'll find out. Sometimes I jist have to say 'Hey you' and point, you know, except I don't do that to Mr. Beck." Another wink and the stream of conversation rumbled into a laugh that agitated her apron.

"Everyone has always called me Renny," Renny said, but as soon as she spoke she flushed, for she found she had addressed herself to the wall. Mrs. Beck had disappeared into a doorway on their right. Miss Kistner patted Renny's shoulder and they followed. In the living room the boy with the airplanes was now on his stomach in front of the TV. Superman blared, the cartoon figures jerking spasmodically across the screen. "Lorrene. . . ."

"Lorraine," Miss Kistner corrected.

"Oh, yes, Lorraine. This here is David." Mrs. Beck prodded the boy in front of the TV with a sneakered foot and he looked up and grunted. "And that's Ralph." Mrs. Beck nodded to a boy on the other side of the room, deeply absorbed in a book. He was blond and doughy-looking, and he wore thick glasses. When he stood up Renny could see he was about her age.

"Pleased to meet you." He gave a slight bow in Renny's direction. She had the impression that if he had been wearing a hat he would have tipped it, like a little old man. But he smiled warmly before he sat down and returned to his book.

"Them two's brothers, but they got taken from their ma," Mrs. Beck said. "She used to beat that little one something awful. He was all purple and green when he came here. Not that he don't need it sometimes. But my husband and me, we don't lay a hand on 'em. Mr. Beck, he jist teaches them the way of the Lord when they're bad. He's a most religious man, my husband. He don't never lay a hand on one of these kids."

Most of the words went past Renny, but Mrs. Beck breezed on.

"And the one with the knobby knees peeking through the door is Karen. She's the littlest and hasn't learned to let people in proper yet." The pale, freckled face disappeared behind the doorway into what was apparently the kitchen. "And where's that Cynthia? Upstairs in her room painting her nails, most likely. Cynthia's fifteen and that's all she thinks about— painting her nails and fixing her hair. That and boys." Mrs. Beck raised her voice. "Karen you scoot upstairs and get Cynthia and tell her to get herself down here. It's time I had some help in the kitchen anyhow."

Karen ran through the room with her head ducked and disappeared up the stairs. In a moment she returned with an older girl moving indolently down the steps behind her. The girl held her wrists out, her hands dangling; apparently Mrs. Beck had been right about what she had been doing. She cracked gum with each step she took. When she arrived in the doorway, she leaned against it and looked Renny over disinterestedly. Karen had dropped behind and peeked out from the hall every now and then.

"Hello, Cynthia," Miss Kistner said. "How are you?"

Cynthia shrugged, still leaning against the door jamb, still cracking her gum. Renny wished she could chew gum like that, but Gram didn't think gum was for ladies, so she hadn't had it very often. She had chewed it a few times when she was with some other kids, but she had never learned to crack it.

"Cynthia," Mrs. Beck spoke, "this here is Lorrene. She's come to live with us. You and Karen can show her the girls' room. Then I want some help in the kitchen before Mr. Beck gets home and wants his supper."

Cynthia turned back to the stairs. Karen stayed behind the doorway, watching Renny. Miss Kistner held out her hand to Renny. "Good-bye, Lorraine. I'll be back to check on how you're doing every month. The Becks will take good care of you. There's nothing for you to worry about."

Renny felt a sudden panic in her throat, as though it mattered that Miss Kistner, whom she had never seen before that day, was going to leave her, as though her last thread with her home and Gram were about to be snapped.

"Miss Kistner, when will Gram be able to come home?"

Miss Kistner's eyes slipped away from Renny's face. "I don't know, Lorraine. We'll just have to see."

"But Miss Kistner. . . ."

Miss Kistner interrupted. "I'll let you know when there is some change, but until then, Lorraine, you have a good home here. I hope you will appreciate it and be cooperative and helpful. Now go along with Cynthia. The boys will help me bring your things in."

Renny looked at Miss Kistner, and the last hope, even the anger that had been shielding her in the car,

7

drained from her. She felt her shoulders sag. She turned to follow Cynthia without another word, and Karen shadowed them.

At the top of the steps, Cynthia disappeared into a doorway to her left and was already bent over her nails with a pearly white polish when Renny and Karen arrived at the door. It was a small room, painted green over wallpaper that had begun to crack and peel, revealing in some places a nursery print, in others bare wall. There were two beds in the room. Cynthia sat on one, her straight blonde hair falling over her face, intent on her nails. A teddy bear, a clown, and a Raggedy Ann doll were propped against the pillow on the other. The only other furniture was a tall blue dresser with chipped paint and a sagging couch under one window. There were no curtains on the window. Karen went to the bed with the stuffed figures on it and gathered them into her arms. "Here," she said, "this will be your bed."

"But where will you sleep?" Renny asked, looking around and thinking of her own blue and white bedroom that she and Gram had fixed up so carefully.

"Oh, I sleep on the couch when we've got another girl." Karen sat Raggedy Ann and the bear and the clown next to one another on the couch. Raggedy Ann immediately fell over, and the clown drooped to one side.

"Thanks," Renny said. "I won't be here long, but I hate to take your bed."

"Take it," Cynthia advised. "The couch would

break your back in one night. Pip-squeak, there, don't know enough to be uncomfortable."

Renny sat down on "her" bed. Karen remained standing before the couch as though guarding it. "Where are you going?" she asked.

"On your way to Chillicothe?" Cynthia interjected.

Renny looked at Cynthia in surprise. Chillicothe was the girls' state reform school. She had heard of that. "No," she answered, surprise and irritation struggling with one another, "I'm going home. As soon as Gram gets well, I'm going home."

"Who's Gram?" Cynthia asked without looking up.

"My grandmother, my great-grandmother, actually. I live with her. I've always lived with her. She reared my mother, too."

"Why?"

"Why what?" The irritation was coming out on top. What right did this girl have to know anything about her?

"Why did she *rear* your mother?"

"Because my grandmother, her mother, died when she was born. My grandfather couldn't be expected to take care of a girl all by himself, so his mother, my great-grandmother did. Anything else you want to know?"

Renny expected the tone of her question to stop the conversation, but Cynthia just smiled to herself and said, still without looking up, "Yeah. Where's your mother?"

"I don't know. She hasn't lived with Gram and me since I was a little baby."

"Illegitimate, huh?" There didn't seem to be any condemnation in Cynthia's voice, just curiosity.

"My mother wasn't illegit. . . ."

"I'm not talking about your mother. I'm talking about you. Any idea who your father was?"

Renny could feel her cheeks growing hot. No one had ever spoken to her in such a way before. Great-Aunt Florence made remarks, but they were always to Gram. Renny wasn't supposed to hear them. Great-Aunt Florence thought that Gram should have turned Renny over to welfare years ago, when she was just a tiny baby and her mother had come back from Chicago with her wrapped in a man's jacket—her daddy's jacket, Gram said. It was dark blue, with a warm, wooly lining.

"Tell me about my daddy," Renny would say to Gram, getting the jacket out and spreading its wide shoulders, its long arms out on the living room floor.

Gram would smile and look up from whatever she was making for Renny. When she sat down she was always sewing. "He is a big man," she would begin, "a big, strong man, and very tall, as tall as the grandfather clock."

"And his hair, Gram. What color is his hair?"

"His hair is very dark, almost black, and it curls. Not kinky curls, soft. And he has a mustache."

"And his eyes? Tell me about his eyes."

"His eyes are blue, blue as the sky."

"And how much does he love me?"

"He loves you so much that when you were a little baby he gave his own jacket for your mother to wrap you in. It was a cold day, because it was February when you were born, and the wind is cold in Chicago in February, but he took off his jacket so that you wouldn't be cold when your mother brought you here to me."

"And tell me, Gram, tell me about my daddy coming to see me."

"Someday your mother and your father will come right here to River Bluffs. . . ." But Renny never listened much to that part of the story. She could tell herself a better one.

Now she glared at Cynthia and answered evenly, "Of course I know my father. I can even tell you what he looks like."

"Oh?" Cynthia's eyebrows made the word a challenge.

Renny drew a deep breath. She had never talked to anyone about her father before. He had been one of her secrets and Gram's. She and Gram had lots of secrets together.

"He is tall . . . ," she began slowly. When she had finished the description, she waited to see what Cynthia would say next.

"Interesting," Cynthia said, going back to polishing her nails. "Sounds like Pop Beck, don't it, Karen?" In the silence that followed Renny tried to breathe slowly and deeply. "What about your great-grandmother? What happened to her?"

"She got sick. They took her to the hospital. I'm going home as soon as she gets well."

Karen spoke up from the couch where she was sitting now, fondling her clown. "My mommy's sick like your Gram. I'm going home when she gets well."

"Huh!" Cynthia didn't so much carry on a conversation as thrust herself into it. She never looked up from her nails. "Don't listen to her. Her mother's not sick, and she's not going to get well. She's mental, looney, cracked. She used to sit all day and rock and cry. The kid, there, told me all about it. Her mother never even knew what she was doing."

Karen's pale face turned chalky, which made each individual freckle stand out as though illuminated. Before she could gather an answer, Mrs. Beck was at the bottom of the stairs.

"Girls, watcha doin' up there? I told you I need some kitchen help."

Cynthia raised her eyebrows, sighed, and capped her polish fiercely, her fingers extended stiffly to protect the fresh coat. She said something under her breath that Renny had heard one of the boys in school say. Renny didn't know girls used that word.

2

FROM the top of the stairs, Renny looked down upon chaos. Her books and games from the box she had packed at Gram's were spread across the hall. One of the suitcases was open. David, the one with the paper airplane, the one who had been purple and green when he came to the Becks, was jumping around, holding her Yahtzee game above his head, and stepping on something else with every move.

"Hey, look everybody. Yahtzee!" he shouted, waving Renny's game like a signal flag, "I've got a Yahtzee game. Wanna play, Ralph? Hey, one of you girls wanna play?"

"Stop that!" Renny said indignantly, starting down the steps. "Those are my things."

"Are they really?" David looked up at her with wide, innocent eyes, and Renny stopped, halfway down.

"Don't listen to that little brat," Cynthia said. "He knows those are your things. He don't have anything himself because his maw never bought him nothing." Cynthia pushed past Renny and went down the stairs.

Renny thought Cynthia was going to rescue her Yahtzee game, but she pushed past David, too.

David dropped the Yahtzee game and the box came open, score papers fluttering everywhere. "Look," he sniggered. He held up a pair of Renny's underpants, pink with red hearts—Gram had just given them to her for her birthday—and began to dance around with them. "Oh, moy," he said in a falsetto, "aren't I something special. I wear fawncy pawnties for all the boys to see!"

"Give me those!" Renny was down the rest of the steps in an instant, her cheeks blazing.

David's eyes glistened and he put his arms through the leg holes and began to clap his hands. "Come see me, all you boys. Come see my fawncy pawnties."

Renny grabbed for the underpants, got hold of the elastic and jerked. There was a tearing sound. Immediately Renny and David were still, staring at one another. Ralph, who had been immersed in his book all this time, looked up, as though the silence caught his attention where the noise had not.

"David," he said, getting up from the chair and coming toward them, "what are you doing with her things? Give that to her!" David began to work his arms back out of the panties.

"What's this stuff?" Mrs. Beck stood in the doorway, her fists cocked on her hips. Her elbows made sharp points beyond the dimpled flesh of her arms. "Whose junk is this anyhow?"

"It's mine," Renny answered. David had dropped

the underpants and sidled past Mrs. Beck and was now watching television as if he had never left it.

"Well, you better get it out of here before Mr. Beck comes home!" Mrs. Beck turned and huffed back to the kitchen, stepping over David with a grunt as she went. "And Karen, you git yourself out here and start helping," she called back over her shoulder.

Karen, who had been standing in the middle of the staircase, came downstairs and slipped past Renny with a sympathetic glance.

Ralph came over and began to pick up the scattered scoresheets. "I'm sorry," he said in a low voice, puffing a little as he bent over for each paper. "I'm sorry David did that. He really doesn't mean any harm."

"He doesn't?" Renny put the torn underpants back into her suitcase and closed it firmly. She looked at Ralph. "What does he mean, then?" Now that her anger was cooling her voice trembled. She began picking up books and games and putting them back into her box. Ralph made no answer, but when everything had been gathered up, he picked up the box and one of the suitcases and started upstairs. Renny picked up the other one and followed him.

When they got to the girls' room, Ralph set Renny's things down carefully and turned to her. "David just isn't very happy . . . with himself. So he does things that bother people."

"I noticed," Renny said.

Ralph took off his glasses and rubbed them on the front of his shirt. Renny could hear a button scratching back and forth across one lens. She grimaced. She had cleaned Gram's glasses since she had been a little girl, and she never would have dreamed of wiping them on anything but the softest, cleanest cloths.

"I hope you'll forgive him," Ralph continued. "He needs people to like him. He really does. He just wanted you to notice him, and he didn't know how to do it." He put his glasses, more smeared than ever, back on.

Renny sniffed, "He sure didn't." But her anger had faded. She looked over this pudgy kid who talked more like Gram than like any other boy she had ever known. His eyes, through his glasses, were a watery blue and magnified so that they seemed to take over his face. He had some acne on his chin.

"What's it like here?" she asked. "I mean, how do you like it?"

Ralph shrugged. "Oh, it's okay, I guess. Mom Beck means well. Pop Beck. . . ." He shrugged again.

"Is that what you call them? Mom and Pop Beck?"

The boy nodded, and then Renny caught a glint of mischief behind his glasses. "Just wait until you break bread with Pop Beck. That'll be a new experience for you!"

A sharp clanging broke into their conversation and Ralph, suddenly serious again, said, "Come on. We have to go to the table," and he started for the stairs.

Mom Beck stood at the bottom landing, shaking an old school bell. Her arm joggled, but her face was intent, beyond thought.

16

In the living room, David was turning off the TV as they passed through. Ralph tousled the younger boy's hair, and when David looked up at his older brother his eyes shone. Karen, who had been setting the dining-room table, hurriedly put the napkins around and took up her place behind one of the chairs on the side of the long, dark table, pointing Renny to the place next to her. Cynthia came in from the kitchen and leaned on the back of the chair on the other side of Renny. The boys took their places across the table. Mom Beck was on the end closest to the kitchen. The head of the table, where all the plates were stacked, was empty. There was no food on the table, and Mr. Beck, Pop Beck, wasn't there. Everyone stood silently, apparently studying the table. Renny looked around.

"Where's . . . ?" she started to say.

Cynthia giggled and nudged her hard. "Shhh! You're supposed to be meditating."

"It aids the digestion, you know," Ralph said in a loud whisper, and the other children snickered. Renny looked around, bewildered.

"Lorrene, we always take a little time before supper, while we wait for Mr. Beck, to think about our sins. Then we'll be ready to pray when he gets home," Mom Beck explained. When she mentioned Mr. Beck she sounded reverent.

"Yeah, and when Pop Beck is late we get more time to think about our sins than we got sins." Cynthia was still cracking her gum. "I begin planning what evil things I can do tomorrow so I can talk about them."

17

The children giggled again.

"Now, now," Mom Beck clapped her hands, but they made only a soft padding, "what would Mr. Beck say if he was to come in and hear you all like this?"

"He'd have something more to pray about," Cynthia muttered, but no one laughed this time and a heavy silence descended.

Renny stared at the wallpaper, blue with white ribbons and bows up and down it, and down at the dark wood in front of her. She examined her hands. Her fingernails were chewed off. Her fingernails were always chewed off. She looked across the table at David's dark head and at Ralph's blond one. Funny to think they were brothers. They were so different. David was fidgeting with his knife and spoon, making occasional small motor sounds as he moved them around on the table in front of him. Renny looked down at the wispy ends of her own brown hair.

A car pulled up outside. David put his knife and spoon down with a clatter. Cynthia quit cracking her gum. The silence was complete this time except for the thumping of Renny's heart. She looked around furtively. Surely the others could hear, too, but they didn't seem to notice. A tall figure moved into the room. Renny kept her eyes averted. She stared at her napkin until it took on the form of a snake and seemed to writhe next to her fork. She blinked her eyes.

She looked up as far as her eyebrows and could see David's perfectly still bowed head. She dropped her eyes again quickly. The voice began, rich and melodious and deep.

"Our Lord Jesus Christ, creator of the world, savior of our poor worthless souls, we thank You for this day and for Your grace, which alone makes it possible for us to have life. We thank You that Ralph and David have been made a part of this home of Yours, away from the terrible tyranny of drink and of brutality. We thank You for having taken Karen out of a home filled with ungodly sickness and for having brought her here into the light of Your love. We thank You for saving Cynthia from the horrors of incarceration and for giving her a new chance to live in Your love."

The voice reverberated in the room, bounced off the ribboned walls and the floor and the ceiling. It almost seemed to set the windows rattling. Renny sneaked a look at its source and then stood transfixed, forgetting to bow her head. She was staring into the fiercest blue eyes, the bluest blue eyes she had ever seen. Mr. Beck, a tall man with a muscular chest and arms, curly black hair, and an immaculately clipped mustache looked back at her. He went on praying.

"We thank You for bringing Lorraine to us, for bringing her into a family for the first time in her young life. May she, who has never known an earthly father, come to know You, our dear heavenly Father, and to share in the richness of Your love."

Renny gaped. What was he saying? She had a father. Gram had told her everything about her father. Everything! And she had told the other girls.

"And now, Lord," the voice continued, "sinners that we are, we wish to ask Your forgiveness for the great evil we have wrought in Your glorious world, for the stain we have brought Your creation; and we come before You in trembling and fear, knowing that the torments of hell await all who live without full repentance, that fires burn without ceasing to sear the souls who thought to live this life without You, without accepting You into their hearts, and without daily begging Your forgiveness for their wrongdoings." There was a pause, and then the blue eyes were turned to the other side of the table. "Ralph."

Ralph spoke without looking up. "Forgive me for being impatient with my brother." Impatient with his brother? Renny almost gasped.

"David."

"Forgive me for being too hungry to listen to the prayers." Mr. Beck looked more fierce. David kept his head bowed.

"Cynthia."

"Forgive me for going to sleep in my English class." Cynthia was twisting a long strand of blonde hair around her finger.

"Lorraine."

Renny was still staring, still trying to sort out what she was expected to say, and all she could remember from the long prayer was that Pop Beck had said she didn't have a father.

"I do, too," she said.

"You what?" Pop Beck was looking at her, his eyes, eyes as blue as the sky, searching her face, seeing her freckles and her nose that turned up too much at the end and her mouth that Great-Aunt Florence always said was too wide—like her mother's.

"I have a father, a real one." Her words tumbled over one another. "He works on a barge line, on the Mississippi, but I'm not sure which one. He's going to come and get me. Tomorrow maybe. Maybe even right now. Maybe he's at the door right now." She looked across the dining-room table, past the living room, to the hallway where the door was. Everybody turned and looked, too, except for Pop Beck. He never took his eyes from her face.

There was no knock at the door.

3

CYNTHIA snored, surely the most astonishing sound Renny had ever heard. She didn't simply make little snorts and whistles the way Great-Aunt Florence did when she sometimes took a nap in Gram's spare room; Cynthia positively bellowed. Renny lay in the darkness feeling as though the walls were shaking around her.

"Sleep in peace," she whispered to herself. That's what Gram always said, but neither sleep nor peace arrived at her bidding.

She hadn't meant to say that about her father. She had never told anybody, not even Gram, about her father getting off one of the barges that locked through the dam just below Gram's house. She'd just known for almost as long as she could remember that that was how he would come.

Gram's house was on the bluff, overlooking the dam. During the winter Renny and Gram could count the eagles that came to the open water to feed; right from the kitchen window they could count them. Then when the ice broke up, they could watch the barges locking through. The men on the barges would be doll-like with distance. Renny could see them, though, stepping from barge to barge, throwing out ropes and pulling them in. Sometimes one of the men would leave the tug and walk up the path along the bluff toward town, and then Renny would wait with her heart pounding, hiding her excitement from Gram.

She knew one day one of those men would walk right through Gram's gate and up to the front door, and he would knock sharply, and when Renny flung open the door, he would say, "You must be Lorraine. I am your father."

Gram was waiting for Renny's mother, but Renny wasn't. When you had Gram you didn't need a mother around to share her with. Renny had seen pictures of her mother. There was one where she sat smiling, without any front teeth, from the piano stool and another, all solemn, in an eighth-grade graduation gown. There was a funny one with her mother sitting in the swing on Gram's porch, her hair pulled back into a ponytail and her jeans rolled up to show thick white socks. It was hard to think of that other child as her mother. A father, though, a father was different. Every girl had to have a father.

Cynthia was wrong. Her father had nothing to do with Pop Beck. And Renny had nothing to do with anybody here. She wasn't even going to stay. She was going to go back to Gram. She had to go back to Gram, or her father would never know where to find her. She sat up in bed, weighing the heaviness that filled her when she tried to think about her father and

23

instead Pop Beck slipped into his place—Pop Beck praying, Pop Beck talking about sin. It was then she heard the whimpering for the first time.

"Karen," she said, speaking toward the faint grayness that was the window above Karen's couch. "Karen, what's wrong?"

There was no answer, so Renny got out of bed and, moving cautiously across the cold floor, reached the couch. Kneeling, she felt for the younger girl and touched her wet face. "What's wrong, Karen?"

The whimpering turned immediately into sobs. "I want my daddy," Karen answered, and Renny took the little girl into her arms.

"Come on. Come get into bed with me. Then it'll be better." Settled back into her bed Renny asked, "Do you know how to sit in a lap in bed? That's what Gram and I used to do sometimes when I was little like you." Karen nodded, and the two girls snuggled together, their heads on the lumpy pillow. Renny smoothed Karen's hair back. It always seemed to be in her face. She was beginning to feel warm and sleepy for the first time. Cynthia turned over and started snoring again.

"I told her once that she snores, but she won't believe me," Karen whispered. The two girls giggled.

The next morning was slate gray and occasional snowflakes scuttled in the wind. They didn't seem ever to touch the ground. Renny, standing at the end of the lane waiting for the school bus with Karen and Ralph and David (Cynthia took an earlier bus to the junior high school), turned her back to the wind. David was stomping on some ice in the culvert beside the highway while Karen and Ralph watched him. Ralph, who had sat over his breakfast cereal reading a book, turned from watching David and came over to Renny, his nose and cheeks and chin bright red.

"I'm sorry about last night, Lorraine." He looked at her squarely and Renny looked at her shoes. Gram would have wanted her to wear her boots for warmth, but since Mrs. Beck hadn't said anything, she had left them at the house. "I should have told you what it was going to be like; then you would have been ready."

Renny didn't say anything for a moment. She stood looking down the highway, but there was no sign of the school bus. At home she walked to school, just a few blocks away. At home she went to a different school, too. She and Miss Kistner had crossed some kind of invisible line coming here, and that meant she had to go to a school in Prairieville, another small town, but not on the river.

"Is it like that every night?" Renny asked finally.

"The prayers, you mean? And confessing your sins? Yes, every night."

"Is it always so . . . so awful?"

Ralph shrugged. "You get used to it. It's not so bad. It doesn't mean anything, you know."

"But having to confess something every night. How do you do that?"

"Oh, you learn. The main thing is you mustn't ever

tell anything too bad or you'll be punished for it. One time I said that I had stolen some pencils, and I got sent to my room without supper."

"Had you?"

"Of course not," Ralph said. "You don't think I'd tell something I really did, do you?"

"You mean you lie?"

"Well, I guess you might call it that. I don't think of it as lying though. I just think of it as keeping Pop Beck happy." Ralph smiled vaguely as he turned to look for the bus.

"Isn't that kind of . . . I don't know the word, but isn't it wrong? I mean they're prayers and all."

"Well," Ralph paused to consider this. "The way I see it, if there is this God and He's good like they say, then He doesn't want kids going without supper."

"Oh." Renny felt doubtful. "But what kinds of things is it all right to say?"

"Don't worry about it. I'll think of something for you tonight. I'm quite good at it. I make up things for David most of the time; otherwise he gets himself into trouble the way he almost did last night."

"Do you always have to take care of David?" Renny asked.

Ralph shrugged. "He's my brother." They both turned to watch David, who had progressed from breaking up chunks of ice in the culvert to skimming them across the road. Neither one said anything for a moment, then Ralph asked, without looking at her, "Is your great-grandmother real sick?"

"No," Renny answered quickly, and then after another silence she said, "I don't know. Nobody's told me anything."

Ralph looked over at her. The snowflakes were beginning to gather on his glasses and, with a single accord, he and Renny turned their backs to the wind. Renny hunkered down inside her coat and wiggled her cold toes.

"I was the one there with her," she said. "I was the one who found her and called Aunt Florence. You'd think they wouldn't treat me like a little baby. Gram would tell me, if . . . if she could."

"What happened?"

Renny hesitated, but it seemed all right to tell this boy about Gram. He wouldn't say bad things about how she had lived "a long and useful life," about how "everything comes to an end." "I . . . I'm not sure. I was in the kitchen, making Gram's tea, the way I do every morning. She has a china collection—you know, cups and saucers—and every morning I make her tea and I bring it to her in a different cup. I've done it for a long time. Aunt Florence used to say I shouldn't be allowed to use those cups, but I've never broken a single one, not one."

Ralph nodded as though he understood about Great-Aunt Florence and the cups.

"I picked my favorite that morning. It was two days ago. A Limoges cup with violets in the bottom. Sometimes Gram's already awake, sitting up in bed and waiting for me, and sometimes she's still asleep and I tiptoe across the room and put the cup and saucer down and kiss her to wake her up. We play like she's Sleeping Beauty and I'm the prince, then."

She stopped and looked at Ralph. She could feel herself flushing. She hadn't meant to say that—about Sleeping Beauty—and she wasn't sure she wanted to say anything more, but he was waiting, his eyes behind the glasses solemn and concerned, so she went on.

"She wasn't sitting up, so I tiptoed, real quiet, and put the cup and saucer down on the table next to her bed, but when I went to kiss her . . . ," she stopped. Ralph didn't say anything. "When I went to kiss her she wasn't asleep. Her eyes were open, and her mouth was . . . kind of open, and she was making a funny sound. Like . . . like it was real hard to breathe."

"I'm sorry," he said.

Renny whirled on him with a sudden anger. "Why are you always sorry?"

Ralph grinned. "I don't know. I guess I was just born that way," and Renny laughed, the laugh apologizing for her anger. It seemed as though she was angry with everybody since Gram got sick, but somehow she didn't need to explain that to Ralph.

"She's going to get well," Renny said. "I know she is. And I'm going to be going back soon. Miss Kistner said I needed a family, but Gram is better than any family."

Ralph nodded, comfortably. A yellow bus appeared in the distance. "I'll take you to Mr. Koscetti to register," he said. "He's the principal. Maybe he'll let you be in my room. Come on, David," he called.

Karen ran to Renny's side and took hold of her gloved hand.

The bus smelled familiar and warm, though Renny had never ridden one before. A comforting odor, like a school cloakroom, greeted them as the door flapped open, though the bus was empty except for the driver, who checked the other children's passes and grumbled something inaudible when Ralph explained, "This is Lorraine. She's new. She'll have a pass tonight when she comes home."

The four children, holding each seat for support because the driver had started up the moment he had seen the last pass, made their way to the back of the bus.

"Since we're the first ones on going to school, we always get the back seat," Ralph explained.

"Is he always so crabby?" Renny whispered, sitting between Ralph and Karen on the long back seat.

"No," Ralph answered, "only most of the time. Don't worry about him. It bugs him whenever we have a new kid without a pass. You'll get one today. When David and I came here he gave us a lecture. Acted like he would be arrested for letting us on without passes. Once you have one, he never pays any attention to you again."

"How long have you and David been at the Becks'?"

"About a year, I guess. The year before we were in three different foster homes. Miss Kistner kept coming and taking us out for a coke to tell us that she'd decided we'd be 'happier' somewhere else. That's a nice way of saying the people you're with don't want you any more. One family was real nice. They were young. David was different there. They liked him." Ralph stopped and gazed at the books in his lap.

"What happened?"

Ralph shrugged and looked at her matter of factly. "They were going to have a baby. They needed our room."

"Oh," Renny said softly, lowering her eyes. "How long will you stay with the Becks. I mean if. . . ."

"If they don't get tired of us?" Ralph flipped the pages of a science book, as though an answer might be found there. David was on his knees on the seat making machine-gun sounds out the back window, apparently oblivious to the conversation. Karen had taken one mitten off and was leaning against Renny, sucking her thumb. Ralph looked up from the book. "Until I'm eighteen, I guess. Miss Kistner sometimes talks about us going back to our mother, but I don't think that will happen. She can't change. I know she can't, and they couldn't do that to David. It wouldn't matter for me. She never hit me anyway. But it would be awful for him. When I'm eighteen I'm going to take David and go out on my own."

Renny was stunned. That was six more years! She had never thought for a moment that anyone could be taken to a foster home and just left there until he grew up. She was glad she had Gram to go back to.

"You'll like the school," Ralph went on, changing the subject.

"It stinks," David interjected. "The teachers stink, the principal stinks, the work stinks, the books stink, the rooms stink, the gym stinks, the floor stinks, the walls stink, the windows stink." He looked briefly pensive. "No. I kind of like the windows." And he trained his imaginary machine gun on a group of children climbing up the steps into the bus.

"I really hope you can be in our sixth grade," Ralph said. "Miss Conners is pretty neat."

Karen took her thumb out of her mouth. "Not as nice as Mrs. Bailey. She's the nicest teacher in the whole world," and her thumb slipped back into her mouth.

They rode for a while in silence, and when the bus came to a lurching stop in front of an old brick building with high windows and arched doorways, Renny's stomach seemed to settle somewhere below her knees. Karen kept hold of her hand, and Ralph said, "Come on, Lorraine. I'll take you to Mr. Koscetti's office."

"Everybody's always called me Renny," she said as they started down the dark, polished hallway. She laughed unsteadily. "Gram likes birds, so she named me after a wren. Lorraine was just my mother's name for me."

"Renny," Karen mused, "Renny, I like that."

"Okay, Renny, this way." Ralph smiled and Renny tried to smile back.

Karen left Renny and Ralph reluctantly at the door

of her first-grade room. "I'm glad I have a new sister," she whispered, holding Renny's hand, and Renny leaned over and gave her a hug. She had never dreamed of being anybody's sister. Was she Ralph's sister, too? And David's? And Cynthia's?

The halls were filled with students, calling to one another, laughing, talking. No familiar face. Renny hurried to stay close to Ralph, pulling her shoulders in to keep from bumping anyone.

Mr. Koscetti had a potato nose and small eyes. His stomach lay in folds over his belt, and his shirt was pulled taut over his stomach. Renny kept watching the bottom button, waiting for it to pop. He got out a large blue card and began asking her questions.

"Name? Birth date? Where did you attend school last? Father's name?"

At this last question Renny stopped short and looked at Ralph. "He means Pop Beck," Ralph explained and gave the information himself. Renny sighed her relief.

When it came time to go to class, Renny was not put into Ralph's class but into another sixth-grade room. Renny, feeling the eyes of the class on her, shifted uncomfortably as Mr. Koscetti introduced her to her teacher, Mrs. Schultz.

"Class," Mrs. Schultz said, clapping her hands for silence because a general buzzing had started up the moment Renny had come into the room, "this is Lorraine Morrison. She comes from River Bluffs, but she's going to be with us now. Aren't we glad to have her?"

Renny didn't know whether anyone else was glad or not, but she was glad when Mrs. Schultz pointed out a seat at the end of the third row and she could sit down.

Renny sat in the back of the room watching her classmates, not so different from the ones in her class at home. When a girl with shining black hair brought her a pile of books and plopped them on her desk without even looking at her, Renny suddenly felt very tired. She tried to concentrate on arranging her desk. Was her teacher in River Bluffs emptying out her old desk this morning? And what were they going to do with her pens and colored pencils, her protractor and ruler and compass, and the new pencil case Gram had bought her? She placed next to one another the two stubby, knife-sharpened pencils Mom Beck had given her that morning, and arranged her books in neat stacks. Mom Beck had patted her arm when she gave her the pencils. Gram always kissed her goodbye at the door, even if someone was waiting for her and she wished she wouldn't. Pop Beck hadn't been at breakfast.

Mrs. Schultz was starting a math class, and Renny found her math book and the page, but she sat with it open, watching the classroom door. Even here her father might come . . . looking for her.

Renny slipped lower in her seat, and a warm cloud settled around her. She didn't see the teacher or the other students, and the recitation came to her faintly, as if from a great distance. She felt almost happy.

4

THAT evening Renny peeled the potatoes and boiled them while Cynthia sat on the kitchen stool and filed her nails.

"I'm glad you're here," Cynthia remarked. "Doing that stuff just ruins my hands."

Renny looked down at her own stubby fingers and smiled. "I like to cook," she said.

"You can have it. When I get out of this hole, I'm never going to touch a potato again."

"What are you going to do?" Renny rinsed a potato she had finished peeling and cut it into the pan.

"What do you mean?"

"Well, like when are you leaving? Where will you be going? Back home?"

"Home!" Cynthia snorted. "I wouldn't go back there if they paid me!" A moment of silence and then she added, "And nobody's ever paid me for nothing."

Renny picked up another potato. They had been in the refrigerator, and her hands ached with the cold.

Cynthia put her file into the back pocket of her jeans, standing up to slip it in and then sitting down again. "There's this guy," she said, but she left the sentence hanging and began scratching at something that had once dripped down the front of the stove and was now hard. Renny finished the last potato and ran a small amount of water into the pan.

"Where's the salt?" she asked.

Cynthia shrugged. "There's this guy, but he's in the pen now."

"Where?" Renny found a salt shaker behind several cans of beans in the cupboard.

"The pen." Cynthia, who had been carefully making marks on the gray linoleum with her heel, looked up at Renny and added, "The penitentiary, stupid. Where've you been all your life? Oh, that's right, with your gramma. Well, he's in the state penitentiary."

"What did he do?"

"Robbed a gas station. Eight lousy bucks to split two ways and he gets sent up."

"Where'd you meet him?" Renny was rummaging through some pans, trying to find a lid for the pot of potatoes. The only one she could find didn't fit very well.

"In jail." Cynthia licked the tip of her finger and dipped it into the sugar bowl.

Renny began looking for a can opener to open a can of peas. So that was what Pop Beck had meant the night before by "incarceration" when he had prayed for Cynthia; she had been in jail. Renny found a can opener, but it needed washing.

"And if you're wondering how I got put in jail, I didn't do nothing. I ran away, that's all. I ran away from my stinking stepfather and my old lady, and for that they put you in jail." There was silence for a few moments.

"How did you meet the guy?" Renny asked after she had the peas open. "Were you in the same room . . . cell?"

"Of course not, dummy." Cynthia went back to filing her nails. "When you're a juvenile you're supposed to be 'out of sight and sound of any adult prisoners.' I know because I heard old lady Kistner say that. Boy, was she mad when she found out I'd met Bill. That's why she hurried and brought me here, because of Bill, but it didn't matter. He was going up to the pen in a few days anyhow."

Renny leaned against the sink and watched Cynthia. As the older girl talked, a soft dreaminess took over her face. "Bill and his friend Goober were in one cell upstairs and I was in the other. Have you ever been inside the jail in Prairieville?" Renny shook her head. "No, of course not, your gram wouldn't let you dirty your little shoes. Well, there's two cells upstairs and then the big tank downstairs. I was in the one upstairs by myself, ya see. The only time you see anybody is when they bring you the crummy food they feed you. Is it ever bad! Or when you have to go to the john. You gotta pound on the door if you need to go to the john any time except when they bring you your meals, and then half the time they don't hear you. At night they don't never hear you. I think the guy who's on at night sleeps or something."

"Weren't you scared?" Renny asked, but Cynthia didn't seem to have heard.

"After a couple of days they brought Bill and Goober up and put them in the cell next to me. I saw them when they was brought in. There isn't anything to do when you're in there except sit on the bed or look out the window into the alley or watch the bugs. When I stood on my tiptoes I could see through the bars on the door and see who came up the steps, so I saw Bill once. Twice I saw him looking through when they was taking me out, and he winked at me."

"But how did you get to know him if you only saw him three times?"

"There was a door between the two cells, a big metal door, and it was locked, of course, but there was a crack along one side of it big enough to slip a piece of paper through. I asked Miss Kistner for the paper and a pencil, and she brought them to me. She even brought me some stamps. I kept those. Huh! Who would I write letters to? And Bill got a pencil from the dumb little guy who brought us our meals. I don't think they ever knew what we was doing. Or maybe they didn't care. I don't know. But we wrote notes back and forth. That's how I got to know him." There was a long silence during which Renny checked the potatoes and turned the flame under the peas down; then Cynthia finished. "Bill's gonna come get me when he gets out. He's gonna marry me and take me away from here, away from the whole stinking place. We're going to California. Bill's got friends in California."

37

Mom Beck appeared in the doorway. "Time to come to the table, girls. Have you checked the roast?" Cynthia jumped up from the stool and opened the oven. Mom Beck picked up the old school bell and began clanging it, her arm shaking more than the bell.

When everyone was at the table except for Pop Beck, Renny began to worry. A sin. She had to think of a sin. She looked at Ralph, imploring. He had told her he would help. Mom Beck went into the kitchen for the napkins which Karen had forgotten to put on the table.

"Ralph," Renny whispered, "what will I say?"

"Say you didn't pay attention in reading class," Ralph answered.

"But I like reading class," Renny whispered back desperately. "That's my favorite."

Ralph smacked his forehead with the palm of his hand. "You're missing the whole point! Try math, then."

Renny nodded as Mom Beck came back in with the napkins. That would do. She hadn't, after all, paid much attention in math class. Was that a sin? No matter. She stood quietly behind her chair, gazing at the dark tabletop. There were toast crumbs on it.

When Pop Beck came in she didn't look up. She could see him in her mind anyway, without looking. It was as though there had never been a time when she hadn't seen him. His voice was almost like music. Listening to him was like being in church, if you didn't listen too closely.

Renny thought of what Cynthia had told her. It must be terrible to be alone in jail. What was Cynthia's mother like? And her stepfather? Maybe she had to run away. And Ralph and David. It must be better for them here than in their own homes. And Karen. Renny looked down at the bent head beside her. She touched the little girl's arm, and Karen moved imperceptibly closer to her.

The math sin wasn't hard to say. In fact, a wave of good feeling washed over Renny when she had said it. Tomorrow she would pay attention in math. Ralph was wrong about making things up. There was enough time in any day to need to be forgiven for something.

Renny closed her eyes, and Pop Beck's voice flowed over and around her. She imagined that he was her own father, that he had found her, that he had felt sorry for the other children and taken them in.

When the prayers were over, Renny realized that she was famished.

After the supper dishes were done—Cynthia had sat on the kitchen stool twisting a dish towel while Renny and Karen did the dishes—Karen asked eagerly, "Wanna play dolls?"

"I'm too big for dolls," Renny answered. "How about cards? I've got some cards up in our room."

"I don't know how," Karen replied doubtfully.

"I'll teach you how to play war. That's easy."

When Renny went up for the cards, Cynthia was already upstairs, sitting on her bed brushing her hair.

She watched Renny get her box from under the bed and pull out a pack of cards. She smiled secretly, but she didn't say anything except, as Renny got to the door, "That's the last you'll see of those."

"Of what?" Renny stopped and turned around.

"Those cards."

"Why? What do you mean?"

Cynthia shook her head. "You'll see," was all she answered, and Renny, irritated, turned away. If Cynthia was going to act so mysterious, she wasn't worth paying attention to. In the living room, Mom Beck was sitting in a large chair in one corner watching the television on the opposite side of the room. David lay on the floor, drawing a picture and watching the TV at the same time. The drawing seemed to be a war picture with stray arms and legs flying out of great puffs of smoke and fire. Renny noticed that one of David's eyelids twitched whenever he was still for very long. Ralph was in another chair reading a book, and Pop Beck was sitting in the middle of the couch engrossed in a newspaper.

"Here they are," Renny said.

Karen beamed.

"Oh," David said, looking up, "I want to play, too. Please can I play? Can I, huh?"

Renny hesitated, but she glanced over at Ralph and answered, "Okay."

"I wanna deal. Let me deal. I'm a real hot-shot dealer."

Renny handed David the cards reluctantly. "All right," she said. "Deal them out three ways."

David took the cards and, bending over them with great concentration, his tongue between his teeth, dealt them out. Renny explained to Karen how to play war. David said he already knew how to play, he knew at least two-hundred card games, but Renny noticed that he listened to the instructions nonetheless.

The three of them played quietly for some time. David started out with both jokers and several other high cards, so he gained steadily on the two girls. Then David and Renny started a war with threes. After they each laid a card face down, they both turned up jacks. Licking his grimy thumb, David laid down another card face down and grinned when he turned up the king of hearts. Renny put down her hidden card and turned up an ace. David stared at Renny's ace, then very slowly he turned over the hidden cards he had lost. One was one of his jokers. His face grew red.

"You cheated," he said. "I know you did! You knew my joker was in there, and you cheated."

"How could I have?" Renny asked with a laugh, reaching for the cards. David scooped the cards ahead of Renny's hand and, before she could say any more, flipped them over his shoulder.

"I quit," he said, but he didn't move.

"You're a little brat," Renny hissed at him, reaching to pick up the scattered cards. *No wonder his mother beat him*, she thought. *Who wouldn't?* She was counting the cards to be sure she had them all when she saw Pop Beck, his paper lowered, and the king of hearts held delicately between his forefinger and thumb.

"What is this?" he demanded.

Renny stammered. "A king, sir."

"A what?" he asked.

"A king. A card. You know." Renny felt helpless. Pop Beck's eyes were sharp blue lights. One corner of his lip lifted and his mustache quivered slightly.

"A card? A playing card? You brought those instruments of the devil, of gambling and degradation into my house? Is this what you learned from your grandmother . . . this, this evil?"

Renny quavered. "Yes. I mean, no. I mean, we never gambled. We just played cards. It wasn't evil."

"Wasn't evil!" Pop Beck was on his feet, the card held at arm's length as if it were foul-smelling. "Why, you poor innocent. Don't you know? Babies going without milk, children without shoes because their parents gamble away their earnings, the very food and raiment of their own children, with these . . . these . . . these harbingers of ruin." Pop Beck was beginning to shake all over, but his hands were very calm when he took the card and tore it down the center, then across, then into bits like confetti. Mom Beck looked up once from the TV, but then she turned back to it as though everything were perfectly ordinary.

"Come here, child," Pop Beck said, his tone suddenly softening; and standing there in the midst of the scattered bits of paper, he held out his arms to Renny. "Bring me the rest of the cards."

Renny hesitated, glancing around the room, but there seemed nothing else to do. David and Karen were still sitting on the floor, looking from Renny to Pop Beck. Ralph had let his book drop to his lap, but he didn't look up. Renny got up slowly and moved the few steps to Pop Beck, holding out the rest of the deck of cards. She had another one upstairs. This was half of a canasta deck, but she wasn't going to say that. Pop Beck took the cards and dropped them into the pocket of his suit jacket. "I'll take care of them later," he said with a smile. Renny started to step back, but he sat down on the couch again and repeated, "Come here, child." She took another hesitant step, and he took her hand and drew her down next to him on the couch. He put one arm lightly around her shoulders. Renny kept her spine stiff and straight, and she stared across the room. "You don't know much about us yet, do you?" His voice was very gentle, more gentle than she had known a man's voice could be. "You don't know, even, why you're here, do you?"

"Because my gram is sick," Renny replied immediately. That was easy.

"No." Pop Beck shook his head slowly. "That is only the reason you are no longer living with your great-grandmother. It doesn't explain why you are here instead of in any one of a hundred other homes . . . or in an institution."

Renny tried to think of the hundred other homes she might be in, but they all came out looking like the Becks', and as for an institution . . . she couldn't begin to imagine. Chillicothe?

"The Lord never saw fit to give Mrs. Beck and me

43

children of our own," Pop Beck continued, "and for a long time, we didn't understand why He was saying no to us, but then we saw the light. I saw it, and when I shared it with Mrs. Beck, she saw it, too. If we had had our own babies, we might have brought two or three beings into the world, but if we could reach out and touch the lives of children such as yourself, children in some great need, we could be part of a much greater plan, a far more important birth. The real birth isn't the one that happens to your body, Lorraine, it's the one that takes place in your soul, and that's why you are here, so that you may come to know the Lord and to walk in His ways. That is the work the Lord has given us to do . . . and you."

Pop Beck gave Renny's shoulder a squeeze, and she looked down at her folded hands. She didn't know what she was supposed to say. She could tell him that she'd never noticed she'd been without the Lord, that she'd never thought much about having to find Him. But no, she didn't think she would say that.

Pop Beck ran his hand down her arm and concluded, "Now . . . you understand." It wasn't a question.

Renny nodded and got up awkwardly. She hardly noticed that Karen followed her up the steps to their room. Her shoulder still felt warm where Pop Beck's hand had been.

5

"POP BECK, Pop Beck." Renny was sitting in the middle of the stairs, dusting the uprights of the banister. "That's all anybody talks about around here. You'd think he was God or something."

Ralph, who was coming down the steps with an armload of soiled sheets, stopped and sat down next to Renny, leaning his chin on his bundle. "Have you ever considered the possibility that he might be?"

"What?"

"God."

Renny threw her dust rag at Ralph but then retrieved it and went on dusting. "Do you have a father?" she asked, after a moment. "One you remember, I mean?"

"Yeah," Ralph said, still hunched over the sheets. "I remember my father. Mostly I remember my mother yelling at him. He seemed to grow littler every time she opened her mouth. When he went away, I used to think she had eaten him."

"Really?"

Ralph shrugged. "I don't know. Sometimes it's hard to know what *really* is."

45

Renny moved down a couple of steps and Ralph bumped down after her. "My father really is looking for me," she said, concentrating on the dust in the cracks. She didn't look at Ralph, and Ralph didn't say anything. He just gathered up the pile of sheets and stood up.

A knock sounded at the front door. Ralph started down the steps, but Renny jumped up, almost bowling him over. "No," she said. "I mean, I'll get it." She hurried down the stairs past Ralph, and she could feel him watching her as she opened the door. A slight, sandy-haired man stood on the porch, holding his hat.

"Hello, Mr. Rawls," Ralph said from behind Renny, and the man smiled pleasantly, but he was looking past Renny and past Ralph, too.

"Daddy! Daddy, Daddy, Daddy." The cry came from the top of the stairs, and Karen skittered down the steps and bolted past Renny, who stood without moving. "Daddy!" Karen exclaimed again, throwing herself into the man's arms. "Oh, my daddy." The man didn't say anything. He just held the little girl and beamed. Renny turned abruptly and climbed the stairs, picking up her dust cloth as she went. She began dusting the windowsills in the girls' bedroom with great energy.

Pop Beck sat at the aisle end of the pew on Sunday. Mom Beck sat at the other end flanking the five of them. Renny looked around. It didn't seem like church. Windows of clear glass gave a view of the

46

stubble of a cornfield. There was a general buzz of conversation, people greeting one another in the aisles. In Gram's church there were stained glass windows and people were silent waiting for the service.

David was fidgeting, moving hymn books around. Pop Beck frowned, and the little boy subsided, hunched back in his pew. After a while he began walking his fingers down the pew. Renny watched him, imagining the sound effects which must be going on inside his head. Cynthia slouched next to Mom Beck, examining her nails, studying the ends of her hair, smoothing her skirt. Karen leaned against Renny. She had cried the evening before when her father had left, and Renny had taken her to bed with her again. Now she sucked her thumb and played with Renny's fingers with her free hand. Renny could hear Ralph breathing. She wondered if he could hear her.

A fat lady in a bright red dress came out of a door in front and sat down at a piano. Renny wasn't familiar with the hymn, but the melody was simple and bright and it made her feel better than anything else had lately. The rhythm of the music moved through her when they all stood up to sing. It pulsed deep inside her abdomen and came out through the soles of her feet. After they finished singing that hymn they sang another. And another. As they sang Renny looked around. Some people sang with their eyes almost closed, swaying to the rhythm of the music, smiling even as they sang. Some raised both arms to the ceiling as though reaching for something . . . or receiving something. Renny glanced up and down the row of children. Karen watched everything with round, solemn eyes. David was swaying a little in time to the music. Ralph, who was looking around also, caught Renny's eye, grinned and shrugged. Cynthia had her eyes closed, and her cheeks were slightly flushed. She looked more peaceful than she did when she was asleep. At least she wasn't snoring.

Mom Beck was shifting her bulk from one foot to the other, not quite in rhythm to the music. But Pop Beck, who was singing in a booming voice, raised his arms and called out "Praise the Lord" at the end of the third hymn. Renny felt herself blushing. Surely everyone would be looking at them, but no one turned around.

"Halleluja. Praise the Lord," came from another part of the small church.

A man was standing in front of the congregation now. There was no pulpit, no altar as there was in Gram's church. The man began a prayer, and his voice rose and filled the wooden building. It was like listening to Pop Beck, only louder and even longer, and he didn't look like Pop Beck. His brown hair was combed smoothly, very close to his head, and his face had a round, scrubbed look.

As he prayed, a murmuring began in different parts of the church. "Praise Jesus" came from behind Renny. "My Savior, my Savior" from somewhere off to the side. A woman's voice close to the front cried out, "I am a sinner." And still the prayer went on.

The murmuring gathered and rose—most of it Renny couldn't distinguish as words—and fell back again as the prayer ended. When Renny sat down her arms were covered with gooseflesh.

The pastor began to call on different people in the congregation, and each one stood up with something to say. "I thank God every moment for my Savior," the first one began. Renny squirmed in her place and wondered if she had ever thanked God for Jesus. She had always known about Him, of course. She had gone to Sunday school as long as she could remember, and to church with Gram. She had heard a lot about Jesus, but she had never spent much time thinking about Him.

Men in dark suits took up a collection and everyone sang another hymn. This hymn was about Jesus, too. Then the pastor began to talk. His voice rose again and filled the little church, and Renny found herself drawing back in her pew as though she could get farther away. The words filled her and surrounded her. They pulled at her from the inside.

The pastor called them saints. Everyone who had accepted Jesus was a saint. The world was divided between those who had accepted and those who had not. Those who had not were sinners and would be cast into hell. There was fire in hell, and people who had refused God's only Son burned forever and ever and ever. There would be no end to the torment for those who were not saved, for those who didn't commit themselves now to the Lord.

In Jesus was hope. In Jesus was peace. In Jesus was strength and joy and eternal life. If you gave your heart to Jesus, you would be well and whole. Your sins—all your sins, no matter how black—would be washed away. If you came now to his altar and offered up your life, God would give you all things.

"Come, come to the altar. Give yourself to Jesus. Open up your heart and let the sun in, the Son, the Son of God. You have only to walk those few steps. It isn't far, not far. A few steps to His altar. And your life will be changed. New.

"Doesn't someone want to dedicate himself, herself? Doesn't someone want to rededicate? A saint who has slipped away, away from Jesus. Hell is waiting. The devil is waiting. Waiting to swallow you up forever. Now is the time. The only time. Won't someone come? Come. Give yourself to Jesus. Let Jesus take you, touch you."

The sound rose from the end of the pew that Renny sat in, but she didn't know what it was. Karen hid her face behind Renny's arm. David peered around the girls. A moan, like an animal, guttural and deep. "Jesus. Jesus. I love you, Jesus."

Cynthia stood up and tears were running down her cheeks. Her face was distorted into a grimacing mask, and her mouth was open, like Gram's had been. "Jesus!"

Pop Beck was standing up and stepping over them, and he was holding Cynthia, and tears were running down his cheeks, too. He put his arm around her and helped her out into the aisle, and together they walked toward the pastor. Together they knelt, Pop Beck's arm still around Cynthia. The pastor prayed, and other people came up and knelt, and Pop Beck never quit holding Cynthia.

When church was over, he led her to the car, and they all followed silently. Cynthia kept her head on Pop Beck's shoulder and cried all the way home.

When they got home, Pop Beck took Cynthia upstairs to her room to pray with her. The bedroom door was shut for a long time.

Renny stood on the edge of the frozen field and shivered. Pop Beck was still in the house, sitting on the couch with Cynthia next to him. They were reading the Bible together and talking in low voices. Sometimes they laughed. Cynthia had been saved. Renny shivered again.

The sky was gray, the air biting cold, an occasional small flake of snow sank silently to the ground. Nothing stirred. Renny's breath hung in the air like a miniature fog. The stubbled corn field stretched to her right and her left as far as she could see. The opposite edge of the field was marked by a line of bare trees, a line such as frequently follows the edge of the Mississippi as it makes its way through the Missouri countryside.

"Do you suppose it is?" she asked herself aloud.

"Is what?" The voice was directly behind her, and she jumped.

She turned to see Ralph. David came around the

corner of the house, shouting, "I almost caught one. I almost caught one of those old hens!"

Renny and Ralph both turned to watch David's approach. Renny was relieved to have attention distracted from Ralph's question and quickly hid her annoyance at losing her brief solitude. Was there never a moment for being alone here? And the river might be miles away for all she knew.

"I was thinking of walking out to those trees," Renny said when David had caught up.

"Sure," the boys responded, and they started out, David running on ahead, going zigzag, dropping behind, running circles around them. The corn stubbles were difficult to walk through, stiff and sharp, each of them in its own frozen hill of earth. There was no place flat to step.

"That was really something with Cynthia," Renny said after she and Ralph had walked in silence for a few minutes. "Weren't you surprised?"

Ralph let out a sharp laugh. "Surprised? Why should I be? She does that about once a month. I guess it would be kind of a surprise for you, though . . . the first time and all."

Renny stopped and turned toward Ralph. "But Pop Beck . . . Pop Beck was crying!"

Ralph hunched his shoulders and stamped his feet. "That's part of it. He always cries."

"Every time?"

"Of course. She was being *saved*." His lip curled slightly when he said "saved," and he turned and began to walk again. Renny hurried to catch up.

"But if she's already been saved . . . ?"

"It's called 'being moved by the spirit.' She was renewing her commitment."

Renny's head seemed to be spinning, slowly. "You mean she's done all that before?"

"That's what I said. Don't you believe me?"

"It just seems so . . . so weird."

Ralph laughed again. "I didn't say it wasn't weird, just that I wasn't surprised."

They walked farther in silence, their hands in their coat pockets. David had run on ahead. Renny thought about Pop Beck with his arm around Cynthia and something rose in her throat.

"I haven't noticed that it's done Cynthia any good," she said.

"Why should it?" Ralph asked. "As far as I can see, the only one it does anything for is Pop Beck."

Renny frowned. What did Ralph mean?

"But then, who knows?" he continued pleasantly. "Just think how awful Cynthia might be without Jesus. At least she's pretty quiet for a couple of hours after she answers an altar call."

Renny remembered the rising and falling of the pastor's voice. She remembered the strange feelings that had pulsed through her while she listened to him talk. "Don't you believe in anything?" she asked Ralph, sharply.

"Not much," he admitted with a shrug.

Renny stopped again and faced him. "You mean you don't believe in God? Not at all?"

Ralph shook his head, then he laughed, but his

laugh didn't sound as though there were anything funny. "That's right. That's a sin. I guess I had better report it at the supper table," and he continued toward the line of trees. David was already there. He was trying to climb one of the trees, but they were poplars, too tall and straight for the little boy to get any hold, so he kept sliding back down. Renny hurried to catch up with Ralph.

"But then," she said a little breathlessly, "who made the world? How did it get here?"

"A cosmic accident as likely as not."

"A what?"

Ralph stopped and tried to pick up a cob of corn that had been missed by the corn picker, but it was frozen to the ground. "It just happened, you know." He kicked at the corn. "Certain factors came together and it all happened. I don't see why anyone had to do it."

Renny thought about that. "Well, if you don't think there's a God, what is there?"

"People," Ralph answered without hesitation, "only people." They reached the trees, and Renny sighed. On the other side was another field and another row of trees. Beyond that undoubtedly was another field and another and another. No river at all.

"You believe in people?" Renny asked, gazing across the gray fields.

"No. Not particularly," Ralph answered. They turned and began to walk back. Ralph called to David.

"Where's the river?" Renny asked. The snow was

coming down more heavily now, but there still was no wind.

"The Mississippi?" Ralph was walking backward, watching for David to come.

Renny nodded.

"About ten miles straight ahead," he said, turning in the direction they were moving and pointing.

"Oh." A sudden anger filled Renny, rose in her until she could taste it. "You just won't believe in God because you don't like Pop Beck. It's because Pop Beck likes Cynthia."

"He sure does," Ralph answered, with a wry little smile.

Renny exploded. She didn't know why she was angry or why she wanted to hurt Ralph, who was so gentle and kind, with David, with everybody, except maybe with Pop Beck.

"It's just because you don't have a father anywhere," she said. "Only a mother who drinks too much and beats up little kids. You wouldn't know a real father if you saw one."

Ralph paled. "What makes you talk about people who don't have a father?"

"What do you mean?"

"Well, if that father of yours is looking for you, why has it taken him so long? Anybody could find anybody in twelve years if they wanted to."

Renny opened her mouth to shout, to yell at Ralph, to tell him he was wrong, that her father was most certainly going to come, that Gram had always said so, but David came running from behind and burst between them.

"Come on," he called back, "I'll beat you home."

"That's what you think," retorted Ralph, and he began to run, keeping carefully behind David.

Renny stood in the middle of the bare field and watched the boys' backs. She could feel the snow brushing her face, like a memory of kisses. "You're wrong," she said finally, but the words were only whispered. No one could have heard her anyway, even if she had yelled.

6

WHEN Renny got back to the house she went directly to her room, slipping quietly past Karen, who was watching *The Wonderful World of Disney.* Cynthia was still sitting on the couch next to Pop Beck. Renny sat on the edge of her bed, picking grayish-pink fluff from her blanket.

Ralph was wrong. He had to be wrong. Her father *was* looking for her, at least he was going to look for her some day. Gram had always said he would come. Every time Renny had gotten out the jacket and stretched its long arms across the living-room floor, Gram had told the story about her father. Was that what it had been, a story? Like talking about Santa Claus or the Easter bunny?

But Gram wouldn't pretend about something like that, about something important like Renny's father. She wouldn't have just made him up. She talked about Renny's mother, Shelley, too, and she hadn't made her up. There were all the pictures, and even Great-Aunt Florence talked about Shelley. Great-Aunt Florence never talked about Renny's father, except one time Renny had heard her say to Gram that she doubted

57

whether Shelley knew who the father was. But who could know if her mother didn't?

Renny understood about babies, about how they were made. Gram had given her a book, and she had read it lots of times. But she still didn't understand how somebody could have a baby and not know who the father was. Was it possible she didn't know his name? If that was true, could be true, maybe the man who had been her father had never been told she was born. Or maybe he didn't care.

But Gram, Gram had known about her father, had talked about him. Did Gram pretend? Was it all pretend? Like Renny's own dream of the river and the boats and the miniature figure walking up the path along the bluff?

Renny closed her eyes and she could see her father as clearly as anyone she had ever known, as clearly as Ralph . . . or Pop Beck. Almost as clearly as Gram.

"No," she said, opening her eyes, "I don't have a father." She sat for several moments in the silence of the room, weighing the enormity of what she had just said. She was alone, alone. No father was coming for her. There was no one but Gram, and Gram was sick. Not even her mother was ever going to come back, despite all Gram's pretending. If her own mother didn't want to come back to see her, why should her father come?

How strange it was that the father she had always known about—pretended about—looked so much like Pop Beck. How did that happen? Was that like Ralph's explanation for the way the world was made—a cosmic accident? She wasn't quite sure about cosmic, but she knew about accidents.

"Why," she had asked Gram once, "did my mother have me if she wasn't going to take care of me?"

Gram had smiled at her, a little sadly, Renny thought, and said, "Likely as not you were a bit of an accident, child."

When Gram gave Renny the book about babies, Renny had tried to find out about her mother, but the book wasn't much help. The people they talked about in it were always married, and they had babies because they wanted them. Who had wanted her?

Gram wanted her. There had never been any doubt about that, despite Great-Aunt Florence, despite the way the old ladies who were Gram's friends shook their heads and looked solemn when they saw Renny. Gram would be well soon, and Renny would go back to her. No one would ever separate them again.

And somebody else wanted her—Pop Beck. He liked kids. Anybody who would take strange kids into his home had to like them. It didn't matter that he wasn't her real father. He was her foster father, which was almost the same. And he looked like her father, her imagined father, even if that was an accident. There was nothing so bad about accidents.

Pop Beck had sat on the couch with his arm around her and talked to her. Pop Beck prayed for her every day and forgave her her sins. Pop Beck wanted her to accept Jesus and be saved.

Renny undressed for bed long before Cynthia and Karen came upstairs. When Karen came into the room, she pretended to be asleep. She didn't want to talk tonight. She was making up a dream about Pop Beck.

The next morning Cynthia was in a terrible mood. She yelled at Karen before she was even out of bed, and Karen cried three times before they were through with breakfast and had gotten out the door. Ralph was quiet. Renny wondered if he was mad. On the way to the school bus, David threw a snowball at her that went down the back of her neck, and she called him a miserable brat. Ralph didn't say anything, but she saw his face go closed and tight. She and Karen didn't sit in the back of the bus with the boys.

In her classroom, surrounded by the buzzing commotion that never had anything to do with her, she got out her social studies book and turned to a special picture she had found last week. It was of a river—the caption didn't say it was the Mississippi, but it could have been the Mississippi—and there was a tug far in the distance. At least Renny had decided it was a tug. It was really too small to tell. She moved the boat, with its burden of barges, grandly up the river, but when it came alongside the shore where Renny was standing, the boat was empty. Renny remembered then. She didn't have a father . . . except for Pop Beck.

She leafed through the book, looking for something

else. She found a darling log cabin tucked secretively away in heavy woods. She moved into the picture, opening the door and looking around the cabin. A fire was burning merrily in the fireplace and the kettle was boiling for tea. She was pouring out the tea, pouring it into a big, man-sized cup and putting it in front of Pop Beck. Just her and Pop Beck. Nobody else. Nobody to interrupt them. They sat across from one another at the table, talking about Jesus. She told him about the mean things she had said to Ralph. He prayed for her and forgave her, and there was that warm feeling. Pop Beck reached across the table and touched her hand.

At the dinner table that night Renny didn't mention anything about what she had said to Ralph. She didn't want Pop Beck to be disappointed in her. When it came her turn, she said she had been dreaming in school. She found she didn't want much supper.

Renny got sick during the night. It was the stomach flu, and she knelt on the linoleum floor in the upstairs bathroom and leaned her forehead against the cold rim of the toilet. Maybe Pop Beck would hear her being sick and come upstairs. Gram used to hold Renny's forehead when she threw up. Nobody heard her, though, and nobody came. Karen hadn't even awakened when she got out of bed.

Mom Beck came up to check on Renny in the morning after Karen and Cynthia had gone downstairs. Renny could tell it was her coming. Mom Beck always climbed the stairs with the same foot first, letting the other one catch up, like a little kid, only she hung onto the banister and pulled as she came.

There wasn't much of anything Mom Beck could do for her. If it had been Gram she would have sat beside her bed, with the shades drawn and the lamp turned away from Renny's eyes, and read to her. And when Renny was feeling a little better, they would have played gin rummy and canasta. If she was sick for more than a day, Gram would have driven to the library and gotten her a whole pile of records and another pile of books, and she would have made chicken broth and a thin potato soup and dry toast with a little bit of honey and hot, sweet tea and red jello—red was Renny's favorite. Of course, all that would have been for when she was beginning to feel better. Now she felt terrible. Nothing would have helped now anyway, except maybe the reading. They could have started *The Lord of the Rings* over again.

Sometimes, when Renny was feeling very sick, Gram would just sit by her bed and knit so as to be right there when she was needed. Mom Beck put her smooth, fat hand on Renny's head and clucked her tongue and asked her how much she had thrown up and whether she thought she would throw up again, and then she went back downstairs to get the other kids off to school. Of course, Gram had never had anybody else to get off to school.

Renny lay in her bed and listened to the morning sounds. She heard Cynthia leave, and then the boys with Karen. She listened a long time to see if Pop Beck was still at home, but there was no further sound except for Mom Beck going up and down the basement steps to the washing machine and clumping the iron on the ironing board. He must leave early before any of the rest of them were up. Where did he go? she wondered. She could imagine him selling something. Shoes? Cars? Bibles, maybe.

Renny dozed a little and woke up in time to run for the bathroom again. Mom Beck came up late in the morning with some lemon soda, but Renny couldn't drink it. When she sat up she felt dizzy. Lying in the bed, struggling with the lumpy pillow, she tried to pretend Gram was there, but once when she began to slip into sleep, the remembered face dissolved into that terrible one, eyes staring, mouth moving soundlessly, and when Renny struggled awake, her throat was tightened for screaming. After that she tried not to think about Gram anymore. She felt so empty, as though even her bones were hollow. She lay very still, waiting, but she didn't know what she was waiting for.

When Karen got home from school, she came up to see Renny. She had made her a picture of a fluffy orange kitten with a pointed nose. Underneath the kitten were the words, PLEEZ GET WEL 200N. It wasn't long before Karen was called down to help with supper, and Renny closed her eyes, almost relieved not to have to respond to her chatter. When she opened them, the setting sun cast monstrous, oppressive shadows all around her, but she felt too tired to get up to turn on the light. She wasn't really sick any more, just tired. Besides, looking at the light would have been worse. Renny lay on her back with the pillow over her head.

"Lorraine." The voice was deep music sounding from a great distance. "Lorraine. Are you awake?"

It was her father, her father come to get her. Renny drew in her breath and didn't move. Her heart raced. A hand touched her shoulder.

"Lorraine?"

Renny moved the pillow slowly, and then she was looking up at an immense shadowed figure. She could make out the outline of the dark hair, the broad shoulders. Tears bubbled over and ran down her cheeks.

"How are you, Lorraine?"

Pop Beck sat down on the edge of the bed.

A confused mixture of feelings washed through Renny's body. She went hot and then cold and then hot again. She looked up at Pop Beck. His features were more distinct now. He took her warm, damp hand in his own large, dry ones, and he sat there in silence, waiting for the end of her tears.

"I thought," she sobbed, "I thought you were my father. I almost forgot that I don't have a father, never had a father . . . ever." And she rolled away from him, burying her face.

Pop Beck stroked her hair lightly. His voice was soothing. "You do have a father," he said, "one who loves you beyond anything you have ever known."

Renny's tears vanished. She lay very still and felt the comforting touch. She took a deep, quavering breath and smelled the warm, sharp scent of his skin. He continued to stroke her, very gently, his hand massaging her back. Renny sat up and looked at him.

"God is your father," he said, his hand falling away. "God is always with you. He loves you. He forgives you your sins."

God? God! Was that what she needed? Her head spun violently. For a moment she thought she was going to be sick again, but then the hand returned, stroking, rubbing, and she felt better. She leaned against Pop Beck.

"You must remember, Lorraine, that Our Lord healed the sick, even lepers, with a touch. He had healing in His hands—love and healing—and He touched people and made them well." As he spoke, his hands reached under the back of her pajama top and began rubbing her back, slowly, gently, in circles. "He will touch you and make you well, too."

He lifted her onto his lap. She settled into his surrounding warmth. She had never sat on any man's lap before. It felt good to be so close, so surrounded.

Pop Beck's big hands wiped carefully at her tears, smoothed down her hair, rubbed her shoulders. "Jesus loves you, Lorraine. Jesus wants you to give yourself to Him. If you open your heart and give yourself to Jesus, you will never lack for anything again. You will never be lonely or frightened or lost. He will be mother and father to you. He will be your husband and your child. He will fill you, make you complete, make you happy."

As he spoke, his hands moved down Renny's back, touching, massaging. They felt so good, those hands. Nothing had ever felt like sitting on Pop Beck's lap, melting into him, surrounded by him, safe. His hands, stroking her arms, touching her legs, made her feel so warm.

"If you love Jesus, you will always feel good," he said, and his voice trembled a little. "Jesus loves you, Lorraine. Let Him come to you. Let Him enter your heart."

Yes, Renny thought. *Yes!*

Pop Beck's hands moved down her sides, under her pajama top, and up again, touching the buds of her young breasts. Renny stiffened. Was this what . . . ? She didn't know. He pulled her tightly against his chest, too tightly. She began to push away from him. He was very strong.

"Give yourself to Jesus," he said, and one hand moved down her stomach and inside the elastic of her pajama bottoms.

"No," she said, pulling herself away violently. "Leave me alone!"

"But I want you to feel good," he answered, loosening his grasp but not releasing her. "Jesus wants you to feel good."

"Don't touch me!" She was trying to get away, though her body was flooded with a strange warmth.

"Leave her alone, Mr. Beck, or I'll report you." A shaft of light from the doorway fell across the bed. Ralph was standing there, his hand still on the doorknob.

Pop Beck's hands fell to his sides and Renny found herself sliding to the floor. She caught herself before she fell and stood between Pop Beck and Ralph, trembling. She couldn't look at either of them. She felt dirty, contaminated.

"I was teaching this child about the love of God," Pop Beck said. "I want her to know Jesus."

"Jesus!" When Ralph said the name it sounded like a swear word.

Pop Beck stood and took a step toward Ralph. "Watch yourself, young man. You don't have to be kept here, you know. We have only to give two weeks' notice, and you will be sent someplace else."

"The boy who refused to be saved." Ralph's voice was heavy with contempt.

"You have been refusing, haven't you?"

"Of course," Ralph said, "and I'm keeping David straight about it, too. You and your Jesus talk. It's all phony. You're phony."

Pop Beck raised one arm toward the ceiling as though he were going to hit Ralph, but he didn't. He just shouted. Pointed at the ceiling and shouted. "An atheist? An atheist in my home? Get down on your knees, boy! I give you this opportunity to repent before you are damned for all eternity. Pray that you may yet be saved, that the Lord in His infinite mercy may take away your hardness of heart. Down on your knees. I will pray for your soul."

Ralph did not move from his place in the doorway. His answer was very quiet. He said, "No."

The hand that had been raised toward the ceiling

moved slowly at first, but it slapped Ralph so hard that his head snapped to one side. Ralph didn't move, and he didn't say anything more. There was a moment of silence during which Renny could begin to see the red imprint forming on Ralph's cheek.

Pop Beck was very calm when he spoke. "You will be sent away. I will call your social worker tomorrow."

Ralph, who had been standing looking totally impassive, gave a formal little bow. He had not touched his cheek where the slap flamed. "David will go with me," he said, and he moved out of the doorway.

Pop Beck stood looking after him, then he turned to Renny who was still standing in the middle of the floor. "My child," he said, in a quiet voice, "you have misunderstood me. I was only being a father to you. You are sick. I wanted you to feel good."

Renny shook her head and folded her arms across her chest, trying to control the violent shaking which had begun, but she had no words.

Pop Beck reached out to touch her shoulder, and she backed away. "When you think about it," he said, "you will understand. I would not hurt you."

When he left the room she crawled back into the bed and curled up into a small, tight ball. That night she dreamed of fire that licked around her legs—and higher than her legs—fire that would burn forever. In her dream she cried out, but nobody came to save her.

7

THE next morning Renny stood at the bus stop, shivering inside her winter coat, her teeth chattering.

Ralph looked over at her sympathetically. "You aren't ready to be going back," he said.

"I'm not ready to stay there," Renny answered between her teeth, and she turned away from him. What did Ralph think of her? What could he possibly think of her . . . now? Karen stayed close at her side, but Karen didn't know anything. Renny selected a seat halfway toward the back of the bus, and Karen slid in beside her.

At the end of the day, when she got off the bus and started down the lane toward the Becks' house, Renny's head ached fiercely. Ralph caught up with her. Karen had hurried on ahead to show Mom Beck the art project she had done in school. David was still at the corner throwing rocks after the retreating bus.

"Are you all right?" Ralph asked. "I mean, Pop Beck didn't hurt you, did he?"

Renny walked with her hands stuffed into her pockets, scuffing the frozen ground. "No," she said. "I'm all right." They walked in silence for a moment and then she added, "But what about you and David? Where will you go?"

Ralph shrugged. "Oh, that doesn't matter much."

"Doesn't matter?" Renny turned and stared at him. "How can you say it doesn't matter?"

Ralph started to walk past her, but then turned around. "One place is just like another after a while. You'll see."

"No I won't," Renny shot back. "I won't see anything. I'm going home soon. Gram's getting better all the time. Miss Kistner said they were taking good care of her."

Ralph looked at her steadily, his gaze enlarged and wavering through his glasses, and then he smiled. "I hope so," he said.

Renny started to be angry, to yell at him. He was going to spoil waiting for Gram the way he had spoiled everything about her father. Then she remembered that he would be leaving soon, and she remembered that he had helped her the night before. Her words stumbled. "Thank . . . thank you for what you did last night. I'm sorry he hit you."

Ralph put his hand to his cheek speculatively, as though he could still feel the slap. "I didn't mind," he said, quietly.

"You didn't mind?"

Ralph spoke quickly, looking at the ground. "Look, Renny, I've always known that I'm different from other kids, other guys, I mean."

70

"Different? How?" Renny asked, though she knew. Ralph wasn't like any other boy she had ever met. *Nicer than most of them*, she thought.

"I don't know. I could never do the things other kids do. I never got my clothes dirty, never ran and made noise, never messed with my food, never talked back, never did anything my mother wouldn't like."

"Because she would hit you?"

"No. She never hit me. That's the funny thing. She hit David all the time, because he came along and was just a normal kid, and Mother couldn't stand it . . . because of me, because I'm funny. She thought it was David. He thinks so, too, but I always knew. I knew because I used to think the things he did were neat."

Ralph looked at David who had progressed to larger and larger rocks although the bus was long out of sight. "Anyway," he added, after a moment, "I'm glad I came upstairs."

"I am too." Renny thought of Pop Beck's hands, and she shuddered.

As they approached the porch Renny and Ralph stopped to stare at the old blue Ford parked in the yard. A chicken was pecking at one hub cap.

"Miss Kistner is here," Renny said.

"I know. I saw the car when we got off the bus."

"Ralph, where do you suppose . . . ?"

Ralph turned back to watch David who was running to catch up with them. "Last time we saw Miss Kistner, she said something about our mother being better."

71

Renny threw a swift glance at David, who was drawing near, his jacket trailing behind him in the mud. "But surely she wouldn't make you . . . make David. . . ."

Ralph took David's jacket as he stopped beside them, and began rubbing at the mud it had gathered. "Who knows? If Miss Kistner will bring girls here for Pop Beck. . . ." Ralph stopped in mid-sentence. David was watching Ralph working on the mud on his jacket with casual interest.

Renny ducked her head. She could feel the heat traveling to the roots of her hair. She hadn't done anything. Nothing at all. Then why did she feel so ashamed, as though she would never be the same again?

"Renny, do you want me to talk to Miss Kistner about Pop Beck?" Ralph asked. "I will if you want me to. It's not right . . . your being here."

"No!" The answer was almost an explosion. "Don't say anything to Miss Kistner. Don't say anything to anybody!"

"What about your great-grandmother? Why don't you write to her? You could call her, even."

Renny saw for an instant her grandmother's face from that morning she always tried not to remember, and she shook her head stubbornly. "I wouldn't want to bother her when she is getting well. Besides, it doesn't matter. I'll be going home soon."

Ralph looked at her for a moment and then nodded. He turned, putting his hand on David's shoulder, and started up the porch steps. Renny followed them through the door. They stopped abruptly in the living-room doorway and Renny peered between them. Beside Miss Kistner on the couch was a tight-lipped woman with eyes set in deep shadows.

"Hello, Ralphy," the woman said. And then to David, "Aren't you going to give your mother a kiss?"

David began walking across the living room toward the two women, slowly as though compelled. Ralph remained in the doorway. "Hi, Mother," David said, bending over stiffly and kissing her on the cheek.

The woman looked up into the little boy's face, and Renny wondered if she were going to cry. "Is that all?" she asked. "I know I've done wrong by you, but it's been most of two years. I've paid, being alone for two years. Do you have nothing else to say to your mother?"

David took a deep, quivering breath. "I wanna come home," he said, and he knelt down, throwing his arms around her waist and burying his face in her lap. David's mother leaned over and kissed the back of his head, and when she looked up at Ralph her eyes were shining.

"I've been getting some help, Ralphy. I'm off the bottle. For good. Really. And I'm so lonesome."

"It's okay, Mother," Ralph said, without moving out of the doorway. And then to Miss Kistner, "Should I go pack our things?"

Miss Kistner nodded, and Renny said, quickly, "I'll help," and she turned and started up the stairs just ahead of Ralph.

The two worked silently for some time, after they

got cardboard boxes from the attic. Ralph knew right where they were. They were the same ones the boys had brought to the Becks'.

Carefully stacking David's drawings, which Ralph always taped up to the wall, Renny asked, "Is it going to be all right, going back to your mother?"

Ralph shrugged, but he didn't look up from the drawer where he was gathering mismatched socks. "Maybe she has changed," he said after a moment. "I suppose people do sometimes. Anyway, I'm bigger now. I won't let her hurt David any more."

Supper was quiet without the two boys. Pop Beck prayed for them and for their mother. *I'm afraid they'll need it*, Renny thought, but she didn't look at Pop Beck.

"Eat up," Mom Beck said, looking at Renny's practically untouched plate. "You'll never git strong again unless you eat, Lorrene."

"Mrs. Beck's good food will help you, Lorraine." Pop Beck's voice was quiet and firm.

Renny kept her eyes down. She wasn't hungry.

Renny came awake in the pale moonlight that sifted in the window of the girls' bedroom. Karen was crying, sitting up in the middle of the bed she shared with Renny all the time now. Renny sat up and reached for her hand. It was clammy and cold. Karen began to throw up before she could get her out of the bed.

When it was over, Renny took Karen to the bathroom and washed her hands and face and changed her nightgown and repeatedly wiped away the tears that kept rolling down the small girl's cheeks.

"I want my mommy," she sobbed, over and over again. "I want my mommy to come back and take care of me. She shouldn't have gone away with the baby."

"What baby, Karen? Your mommy is sick. She's in the hospital to get well. You told me that yourself when I first came."

Karen shook her head violently. "No. She went to the hospital to get the baby. That's where the baby came from. And after the baby went away, she went to the hospital again. Only she didn't come back. And Daddy brought me here." Karen began to vomit again.

Cynthia woke up and held Karen on her lap while Renny stripped the soggy, smelly sheets and carried them to the basement. She knew she should carry them all the way down and soak them in the laundry tub, but in the dark doorway her courage failed her, and she dropped the crumpled sheets on the steps and walked back through the dark hall. Mom and Pop Beck's bedroom door was at the bottom of the stairs; Renny hurried past without looking at it. She found fresh sheets and made up their bed again while Karen sat on Cynthia's lap, her tears dissolving into hiccups.

Cynthia found an old enameled bucket in case Karen threw up again. The girls put it beside the bed, and Karen slept on the outside for the last part of the night. As the morning light reached the corners of the room, Karen sat up and began vomiting again. She missed the bucket.

"Oh, Renny," she sobbed, when she had her breath. "Don't leave me. Please don't go to school and leave me."

"Shhh," Renny said, tucking Karen's hair behind her ears and kissing her hot forehead. "I'm not going anywhere. I'm going to stay right here with you."

Cynthia was sitting on the edge of her bed, pulling at her twisted pajamas and wrinkling her nose against the sour smell. Without looking up she said, "He'll be mad at you for sure if you don't go to school unless you're good and sick yourself."

"Who cares?" Renny tossed back, as though it were Cynthia she was angry with. There was no need to ask whom she meant by *he*. "Just tell Mom Beck I'm going to stay home with Karen." And to Karen she said as she tucked her back into the bed before going in search of a floor rag, "Don't worry. I won't leave you. I'll be right here . . . always."

Is there, she wondered, as she searched under the bathroom sink for a rag, *any such thing as always?*

The day lasted forever. Mom Beck didn't argue with her staying with Karen. She brought her a bowl of soggy cornflakes for breakfast and a bologna sandwich for lunch. By lunchtime Karen was sipping some Seven-up and sitting up in bed, but her face had a yellow pallor. The girls had played gin rummy for a while with the other half of Renny's canasta deck. They gathered up the cards in a hurry when they heard Mom Beck coming upstairs, but she probably wouldn't have said anything anyway. Karen slept much of the afternoon, and Renny flipped through old books she could no longer bring herself to read. Mostly she listened for Pop Beck to come home.

Mom Beck sent Cynthia upstairs after school with the suggestion that, since Karen was feeling better, Renny ought to come down and help with supper. Renny shook her head stubbornly. "No," she said. "I'll just stay with Karen. She needs me."

Cynthia leaned back against the door frame and chewed on a toothpick. She watched Renny with knowing eyes, eyes much older than she was, but she didn't say anything.

Renny and Karen had supper alone in the bedroom that evening, and Pop Beck didn't come upstairs to try to make the patient feel better.

When bedtime came, Karen went to sleep easily, but Renny was so restless that she finally took a blanket and moved to the couch, afraid that she was going to awaken Karen with her twisting and turning. She lay on her back on the saggy couch—Cynthia had been right; one night was enough to break a person's back—and watched the stars that barely pricked the darkness. They seemed almost as far away as Gram, as Gram and the father she had never had.

She couldn't think of her father any more. She couldn't even pretend and know it was pretending, because Pop Beck would come between her and the dream and his hands would make her feel warm and then her cheeks would be burning with shame. How awful she must be for Pop Beck to touch her so. He must know something about her, something Gram had never known. And why did his touching feel good when it was also so terrible? What was wrong with her?

She crossed her arms over the beginnings of breasts that she had been so proud of and wished they had never come . . . to be touched. She was beginning to have hair, down there and under her arms. Just a little. It had seemed exciting before, that sign of growing. Now it seemed a burning symbol of her own evil nature. Had Pop Beck's hand gotten far enough to feel the hair? She wished the memory would go away. She wished she could go away, anywhere. She wished she were little again—little like Karen and had never. . . .

Karen. Who would take care of Karen when Renny went back home to Gram?

Karen's father needed to know. He needed to be told to get Karen out of here before something happened to her. But Karen was nice, and she was little. Pop Beck wouldn't. . . . Would he. . . .?

How could she say anything to Mr. Rawls, though? If she told him about Pop Beck, Mr. Rawls would know everything about her. No, she couldn't talk to him or anybody else, either.

Renny turned over and hid her face in the couch. She squeezed her eyes tightly closed. From deep in the darkness at the back of her head she heard Great-Aunt Florence's voice.

"Why do you waste yourself on that child? She'll just be another slut like her mother."

Was that what she was? Was that what her mother had been?

And what was a slut exactly? Was that what a girl was when a man touched her?

8

On Saturday afternoon, after the cleaning was done, Renny went into Prairieville with Mom Beck to shop for groceries. Karen, who had gone back to school with Renny for the last two days of the week, was away with her father again. He came to get her every Saturday. They had left so quickly Renny wouldn't have had time to talk to Mr. Rawls if she had wanted to.

There was a new boy at the house. Miss Kistner had brought him on Friday. His name was Cliff, and apparently he had been in jail before he came, because Pop Beck used the word again in the prayers—"incarceration."

"A fancy word for a bum rap," Cynthia had said, but Cliff just stood with his hands in his pockets and said nothing. He hadn't done much more than stand with his hands in his pockets during the Saturday morning cleaning, either. The cleaning felt like hard work with Ralph not there to talk to, and Renny had found herself doing a halfway job Gram would have been ashamed of.

She wasn't really interested in the grocery shopping,

but it was something to do. She tagged after Mom Beck, who chattered steadily as she padded through the store. She always seemed to have a lot to say when Pop Beck wasn't around. Renny pushed the cart, letting it drift ahead of her and then catching it just before it rammed Mom Beck's behind. Once she hadn't caught it quickly enough, and it had bumped Mom Beck, but Mom Beck just turned and smiled. *Does anything make her mad*, Renny wondered. *Pop Beck or other people's kids or anything?* Mom Beck scratched one arm thoughtfully as she stood in front of a display of canned goods. Renny left the cart and wandered down a different aisle.

He was at the dairy case when she saw him. At first she thought she must be mistaken, but when she got closer there was no question. It was Ralph. He was turning away from her, a half-gallon carton of milk in his hand.

"Ralph," she called, pushing past a woman who was scolding the child squirming in her cart, "Ralph, wait!"

Ralph stopped and turned slowly, as though he expected something bad to happen. When he saw Renny he smiled, but only barely.

Renny hurried up to him. "What are you doing here?"

He held out the carton of milk for an explanation.

"I didn't even know you lived in Prairieville—when you're with your mother, I mean. I didn't see you at school."

"We live about three blocks from here," Ralph gestured in a general way, "and we go to North Prairieville Elementary when we're home."

"Gee, I wish I . . . I mean it would be nice if . . . I sure do miss you, Ralph."

Ralph smiled again, but his eyes didn't smile. "I wish I could invite you to the house, Renny, but I don't think . . . well, Mother isn't feeling too well this afternoon." He shifted the carton of milk to his other hand and wiped the hand that had held the milk on his pants. He looked as though he were ready to turn and go, so Renny reached out and put her hand on his arm. "Ralph, has she . . . I mean are things different for you and David?"

Ralph looked down and backed off a step so that Renny's hand fell away, and when he looked up again, his face was set and hard. Renny took a step back herself.

"Nobody ever changes," he said.

Renny stood where she was and watched Ralph go through the check-out with his carton of milk. His shoulders were slumped under his light jacket, and Renny, watching his back, wanted to rush up to him and touch him again and say, "It's all right, Ralph." But what was all right? Was it all right if Ralph's mother got drunk and hit David? Was it all right if Ralph found out he couldn't stand up to her, even if he was two years older than before, even if he had stood up to Pop Beck?

Mom Beck came down the aisle pulling the cart after her, as though she had considered it too much trouble to walk around to the pushing side when Renny had disappeared.

"I saw Ralph," Renny said.

"Ralph?" Mom Beck looked bemused, as though she couldn't remember who Ralph was. "Oh. That's good." She studied the list in her hand. "I'm glad he and David got back with their momma."

"Yeah," Renny said.

Karen bounded into the bedroom and jumped onto the bed, bouncing several times on her hands and knees after she had landed.

"Oh, Karen," Renny said, reaching out to cover her scattered game of solitaire, "slow down, will you? When did you and your dad get back?"

"Guess what!" Karen responded. "Guess what! Guess what!" and she bounced a couple more times on the bed, ignoring Renny's cards and her question.

"I'm not good at guessing. You'll have to tell me." Renny began to gather her cards. She pried one out from under Karen's hand. At home she had almost never played solitaire, unless she and Gram played double solitaire. Here there didn't seem to be anything else to do, especially while Karen was gone all day Saturday. Besides, it felt kind of good to do something Pop Beck had forbidden, even if he didn't know.

"My daddy is going to take me to St. Louis tomorrow, to the zoo, and then to the hospital to see my mommy. And he invited you to come, too. He's downstairs asking Pop Beck right now. Oh, Renny," she threw her arms around Renny and squeezed until both girls had to gasp for breath, "the zoo and my mommy and you and my daddy, all together. I'm so happy!"

"I'm glad for you," Renny said, beginning to lay out a new game, "but don't get too excited about my going. Pop Beck probably won't let me."

Karen calmed as suddenly as she had rushed in. "But he has to, Renny. If my daddy asks, he just has to. I'll go see," and she was out of the room as quickly as she had come in.

A few moments later she was back, more excited than ever. "You can, Renny. See, I told you my daddy could do it. You can! You can!" She tugged at Renny to get her off the bed and the two girls spun in the middle of the room until even Renny collapsed in a heap of giggles.

She wouldn't have to go to church with Pop Beck the next morning, and maybe she would find some way to talk to Mr. Rawls about Karen. She hugged the little girl tightly and began to rock her.

"In like a lion; out like a lamb," Mr. Rawls said, holding the door against the buffeting wind. "Are you girls brave enough for the zoo this March day?"

"But why do we have to be brave, Daddy?" Karen asked, taking Renny's hand and skipping toward the car.

"Because," he answered, following them, "the wind

is apt to pick you up and throw you into the elephants' cage. What would you do then?"

"I'd hang onto the elephant's trunk," Karen sang, "so it couldn't blow me any farther."

"And what would you do, Renny?" he asked, after they had slammed the car doors and settled into the front seat. Renny concentrated on helping Karen adjust her seat belt. "I'd put chewing gum on the bottoms of my shoes so the wind couldn't blow me anywhere."

Mr. Rawls started the car. "Why, you would really be stuck up, wouldn't you?" he teased.

"No. I'd be stuck down."

"Ooooh," Mr. Rawls groaned. "I think I had that coming."

The highway to St. Louis trailed along the Mississippi. The trees that overhung the river and the road most of the way were still bare, like uneven netting holding back the sky and the river. The ice was beginning to break up on the river now. In some places it had piled up along the shore or against bridge supports. They passed a coal barge moving slowly upstream. Renny was surprised that the sight of a barge no longer made her catch her breath in anticipation. All that seemed a long time ago, the pretending about her father. Had it ever been more than a game? She glanced over at Mr. Rawls. He was watching the road, but one hand rested lightly on Karen's leg. She chattered, to her father, to Renny, to the very air, and as she talked she bumped up against him and nuzzled him like a puppy. Mr. Rawls looked relaxed and happy. He listened attentively, and though he didn't say much he often nodded or patted Karen's leg or gave some other sign of interest and agreement.

Karen talked about everything, but Renny realized, listening to her in a vague kind of way, that the things she said about Pop Beck didn't tell her father much that mattered. If Renny had been talking about him a week ago, before he had come to her bedroom to make her feel better, she wouldn't have sounded any different. She had to talk to Mr. Rawls, but what would she say? Even if she didn't let on that it had felt good, he would know. He would just look at her and know, and then what terrible things he would think. Renny could feel the guilty weight she had been carrying in her stomach all week. It was as though the flu had never quite gone away.

"I want," Karen announced as they piled out of the car into the zoo parking lot, "to slide down the slide in the children's zoo, to ride the train, and to buy a balloon."

Her father laughed. "Don't you want to see the animals?"

"Yes," Karen said, "that too, but mostly I want to slide down the slide, ride the train and buy a balloon."

They did all those things, and they saw the animals, too, and they ate hot dogs and even snow cones. Though the wind was still gusting along the zoo sidewalks, the early March day felt like spring. Mr. Rawls did everything with them, sitting between the two girls and holding them both tightly when the miniature train whistled through a dark tunnel. As soon as the train stopped, Renny stood up, and his hand fell from her shoulder.

The ride was quieter after they left the zoo. Mr. Rawls maneuvered through the increasing traffic. Karen was sucking her thumb. Renny looked out of the window and wondered what Karen's mother was like. Karen's mother was in a mental hospital. Renny had never seen a mental hospital. She had never seen anyone who was sick that way, at least not that she knew of. She wished they could have gone just to the zoo.

They left St. Louis behind, gliding along a four-lane highway. The traffic began to thin around them. There were cows grazing in the fields and litters of little piglets and sometimes some horses. Renny had never ridden a horse, but she had always dreamed of it. She smiled to herself. That was one of the things she had always been going to do with her father, only when he took her to ride for the first time he was going to find that she was an accomplished horsewoman. It seemed silly now, but it had been fun dreaming about it then, more fun than just looking at the horses.

After they turned off the highway and drove through Fulton, where the state hospital was, Renny began to fidget. She wondered if she could stay in the car without seeming rude. When they turned at the edge of town and drove toward a complex of gray stone buildings, tall and stern and grouped tightly together, she slumped down in her seat. Karen, beside her, leaned against her father in silence. Renny wondered if she was frightened, too. But it was *her* mother. Surely Karen wasn't afraid of her own mother.

The wind grabbed at them when they got out of the car. They walked along sidewalks between the looming buildings. Renny looked in one as they walked past, and a man in a business suit stood holding the door open for a lady in a blue dress. Did they work here? Did they know somebody who was a patient here? She got a glimpse down the tile corridor. The walls were white and bare. Everything seemed cold, though the day had been warm. Renny shivered, and Mr. Rawls looked down at her. She didn't want him to know how she felt. She drew in a deep breath and tried to smile. The corners of her mouth twitched, but the twitch didn't feel like a smile.

They entered one of the buildings and Mr. Rawls checked in at the desk. *He has to ask to see everybody,* Renny thought, *his daughter, his wife.*

"She's in the lounge, Mr. Rawls," the woman said.

There were a number of women in the lounge. One was knitting, and two others were arguing in a bantering way over a checkerboard. None of them *looked* sick. Renny hung back in the doorway. She wished she hadn't come. Getting out of church and going to the zoo weren't worth having to come here.

"Mommy!" Karen cried, and she ran across the room, throwing herself at a young woman in a chenille robe who sat by herself, her long, rusty-gold hair falling in a snarled mass below her shoulders. The woman opened her arms for Karen, but she looked across at Mr. Rawls. Her face was a white blank.

"Mommy, Mommy, Mommy," Karen said, but she didn't let go of her to look into her face.

"You're late," his wife said to Mr. Rawls.

"I know I am. I took the girls to the zoo first."

"Girls?" Her expression took on a hint of interest, curiosity. As she spoke she was running her hands quickly and gently all over Karen, feeling her face, running them down her back, caressing her arms.

How beautiful she is, Renny kept thinking, looking into her pale face and eyes that seemed to reflect the gold of her hair.

"Yes. I brought her friend, too." Mr. Rawls motioned for Renny to come forward.

Karen stood up. "Oh, she's not a friend, Mommy. She's my sister. Her name is Renny," and Karen took Renny's hand and solemnly drew her forward to meet her mother.

Karen's mother blanched, and her eyes darkened, but she looked off into the air at a point past Renny. "You don't have a sister," she said.

"I don't have a *baby* sister," Karen corrected, gently. "I can still have a big sister. Renny is my big sister. Oh, Mommy, when are you going to come home?"

Mrs. Rawls looked down at her hands in her lap. They twisted over and over in one another, as though they moved by themselves, without any guidance from

Mrs. Rawls. She sat with her shoulders slumped forward, her back slightly rounded. Renny got the feeling that any movement, except that of her hands, would be an effort too great to be undertaken. "You didn't ask me," she said, focusing her attention on her hands, but from the severe tone of her voice apparently addressing her husband, "about bringing Karen this week."

He sighed and sat down in a nearby chair. "I didn't decide to bring her until yesterday. I thought it was time."

"What about me?" Mrs. Rawls asked tightly. "Did you think what it would be like for me?"

"I thought," Mr. Rawls said very quietly, but with a steel edge in his voice, "that you would be happy to see your daughter."

Her eyes flashed as she looked up at him, but then her face became impassive again, withdrawn. "But you didn't ask me," she said flatly. "You just decide for yourself . . . everything. After the baby died you took that job that keeps you traveling all the time. 'We need the money,' you said. But what good does the money do me . . . here? What good does it do Karen where she is?"

Mr. Rawls ran his fingers through his hair, a frustrated grimace on his face. "It's all my fault, isn't it, Jo Anne? Everything. The pills you took. Coming home to find you half dead, Karen frightened out of her wits, just sitting there by you. Just sitting. Do you know what it was like? Have you ever thought about it?"

Karen had drawn back to stand by Renny when the argument had started, and she was looking from one parent to the other, her face a mirror of pain and confusion. "Stop!" she shouted, finally, reaching out as though to cover both of their mouths and then putting her hands over her own ears instead. "Don't do that!" She squinched her eyes closed, too. She seemed to think the unpleasantness would go away if she could neither see nor hear.

Mr. Rawls stood up quickly and tugged at his jacket, as though rearranging his feelings. "We didn't come here for this," he said, forcing a smile in the direction of the girls. "Why don't we all go for a walk? It's a beautiful spring day. And then we can drive into town for supper."

Mrs. Rawls' hands flew to her hair, touched her robe. "Oh, I couldn't," she said. "Look at me."

"Mommy, please," Karen pleaded. She had uncovered her ears, but she was holding Renny's hand, not moving closer to either of her parents.

"I'll help you get ready, Mrs. Rawls," Renny said, squeezing Karen's hand. "I'm good at doing hair and stuff. I used to help my gram all the time."

Mrs. Rawls looked at Renny intently, her eyes seeming to measure something invisible. "How kind you are," she said, and then she stood, tightening the sash of her robe, and added, almost gaily, to Mr. Rawls and Karen, "We'll meet you on the bench in front of the administration building in twenty minutes."

9

MRS. RAWLS' hair glowed in the lamp light. She sat on the edge of her bed and Renny stood beside her, brushing very carefully. Mrs. Rawls' hair was even prettier than Gram's, though not quite as long. Renny had the snarls out and the hair lay in a gentle wave down Mrs. Rawls' back.

"Your hair is beautiful," Renny said, taking the large barrette Mrs. Rawls offered and drawing it together at the back of her neck.

"I know." Mrs. Rawls smiled apologetically. "I used to take care of it. It used to look pretty all the time. But here—it hardly seems to be worth doing anything, about my hair or anything else."

"Is it awful here?" Renny asked.

Mrs. Rawls shook her head. "Not so awful. It's rather pleasant, actually. Quiet and pleasant. They take good care of me."

Renny thought about Mrs. Rawls being taken care of as she clasped the barrette. Mrs. Rawls didn't seem sick; more what Gram would call moody. If she knew about Pop Beck. . . . Wouldn't she want Karen to be taken care of, too? "But don't you want to go home?"

Renny asked carefully. "Wouldn't everything be better there?"

Mrs. Rawls shook her head again. "It's not so easy, Renny; not as easy as it looks. I'm so lonely there."

"Why?"

"That's where the baby died." Mrs. Rawls spoke without emotion.

"Oh," Renny said. "I . . . that's too bad."

Mrs. Rawls was swaying slightly as she sat. "He blames me. I know he blames me."

"For the baby?" Renny asked carefully.

"For everything. For taking the sleeping pills. He just went away, took that awful new job and left me. It was a whole bottle."

Renny didn't say anything. She ran the brush again through the glowing bronze hair.

"I put the baby in her crib one night, and when I went in to get her in the morning, she had quit breathing. It was hard to believe she wasn't just asleep . . . but she wasn't." Mrs. Rawls' voice faded away, and a heavy silence settled in the room.

"But why do you stay here?" Renny asked after a time.

Mrs. Rawls looked down at her hands and then over at Renny. "Why shouldn't I stay?"

"Because Karen needs you."

Mrs. Rawls looked back at her hands. She twisted her wedding ring around and around. "Karen needs a mother, but I'm not sure it's me she needs. I don't think I'm good for Karen."

"But you *are* good for her. You're her mother. Nobody else can be that." Renny got down on her knees beside the bed so she could look up into Mrs. Rawls' face. "Mrs. Rawls, the foster home where Karen is . . . they don't take good care of her."

Mrs. Rawls' eyes slid away from Renny. "You love Karen, don't you, Renny. You take good care of her."

"Yes, I love Karen, but she needs *you*."

Mrs. Rawls smiled faintly and stood up. "Come on, Renny," she said, "they'll be waiting for us."

They walked around the hospital grounds for a time, Karen fluttering from her mother to her father to Renny like a butterfly, and then, with permission from the charge nurse, they went out to supper.

Mrs. Rawls talked to Karen, asked her about school and about her foster home. *She's trying to find out if what I said is true*, Renny thought, but Karen didn't say anything bad about Pop Beck or about the home. When they took Mrs. Rawls back to the hospital she was silent and withdrawn again, but she hugged Karen before they left. She even hugged Renny. She smelled like violets.

Mrs. Rawls stood for a moment in the dimly lit lobby with its plastic and metal institutional furniture and its antiseptic smell, and she reached out to touch Renny's cheek lightly. Then she turned to Mr. Rawls and said, "Bob, if you ever decide to come home . . . I might . . . I would try. . . ."

He waited for a moment for her to finish her sentence, and when she said nothing more he reminded her gently, "The traveling is part of my job, Jo Anne."

"I know," she answered, and she turned and walked down the hospital corridor, her back very straight.

Karen was asleep with her head on Renny's lap before they were far outside of Fulton.

"I like Mrs. Rawls," Renny said, watching a pyramid of approaching headlights.

Mr. Rawls nodded. "She liked you, too," he said. A comfortable silence filled the car. Renny stroked Karen's cheek. Her eyelids fluttered and then closed again. They turned off the four-lane highway and were moving more slowly on the winding river road. Renny could see the moon wavering from the river.

"She doesn't seem sick to me," she said after a time.

"The doctors say she's getting better. I hope she is. Sometimes," Mr. Rawls hesitated, and Renny thought he wasn't going to say anything more, but then he continued, "sometimes it seems as though she doesn't want to get well."

Renny looked down at the sleeping figure on her lap and enclosed Karen's damp thumb in her hand. Here was her chance to talk to Mr. Rawls. "What will happen to Karen if she doesn't get well?"

Mr. Rawls didn't answer for a moment. "I suppose she will have to stay in foster care. I don't know what else I can do."

Renny spoke without looking at Mr. Rawls. "You can't leave her in a foster home, not at the Becks', anyway."

"Why not?"

Renny could hear the surprise and concern in Mr. Rawls' voice. She could feel him looking at her, but she still didn't turn toward him. "It's a bad place," she said.

"But how is it bad, Renny? What's wrong?"

Renny looked down at Karen, watched her soft breathing, then she looked out the window toward the river. She didn't say anything. What was there to say? He would just have to believe her that it was bad.

"You have to tell me what the problem is." Mr. Rawls' voice was tight and sharp. "I can't do anything unless I know what's wrong."

"Why can't you just take her home? She's your daughter. They can't stop you from taking her home."

"But I have no way to care for her at home. I'm not even at home all week. And if I ask to have her moved to a different foster home, I would have to have a reason. Tell me what's wrong, Renny."

"Why don't you bring Mrs. Rawls home from the hospital? Why don't you stay home yourself?" Renny asked, ignoring the tone of command. Mr. Rawls was worried. That was good. If he was worried enough he might take Karen away from the Becks without Renny having to tell anything.

"Because she's not ready to come home from the hospital." Mr. Rawls sounded exasperated. "Because I have to make a living."

"She thinks she's not good for Karen, but that's not true." Renny remembered the pale, freckled face, so like Karen's.

"I know."

"Can't you tell her that's not true?"

"Did you try to tell her?"

Renny looked out at the reflected moon. "Yes."

"Did she believe you?"

"No."

"Well?"

Renny looked at Mr. Rawls. "But she would believe you."

"Hah!" Mr. Rawls' laugh was so sharp that Karen stirred, but she went on sleeping. "She would probably believe me the least of anybody. She thinks I don't care about the baby because I went back to work, because I had to travel and I left her alone. She even thinks I don't care about her and Karen."

"Do you?"

Mr. Rawls struck the steering wheel forcefully with the heel of his hand. "Yes, damn it!"

"Then why is she by herself in a hospital and why is Karen at the Becks? If you cared about them you'd have them at home. If they'd let me, I'd be taking care of my gram. I wouldn't let strangers be doing it."

"Well, Lorraine"—Mr. Rawls' words were cool and clipped—"I'm glad you have the world so nicely sorted out. You're going to solve everybody's problems, aren't you? Just like that. How long have you been at the Becks' anyway, less than two weeks? What can you know in that little time? Karen has been there for three months, and she has never complained. Of course, she misses me and her mother, but she's never had a bad word to say about the Becks."

97

"Maybe nothing's happened yet."

"What do you think is going to happen? Tell me."

Renny turned to stare out the window again. The moon had moved higher in the sky and was no longer reflected in the river. The river was black and menacing. "I'm afraid he might hurt her."

"How?"

Renny continued to look out the car window. She didn't answer.

"How, Renny?"

"How should I know how?"

"Well, you must know something. What makes you afraid Mr. Beck will hurt Karen? That is who you're talking about, isn't it, your foster father?"

"He's not *my* anything."

"Has he hurt you, Renny?"

"No." She shook her head. Dark skeletons of trees marked the river she could no longer see. She remembered Pop Beck talking about love and about God and Jesus. She remembered his hand that moved in circles up her back and then began to touch more than her back.

"Renny," Mr. Rawls' voice was gentle now, "I know you are very good to Karen and already she loves you. If there is something wrong, I need to know what it is. Then perhaps I could help you as well as Karen. But you have to tell me."

Renny remembered the prickling warmth that had surged through her body when Pop Beck had touched her. "There's nothing to tell," she said.

10

THAT week Renny began to work on a plan. She would take Karen and they would run away. She didn't talk to anybody about her plan, not even Karen, but she was sure that Karen would go with her when the time came.

Renny didn't know why she hadn't thought of it before. Gram's house. She still had her key on the string around her neck. She and Karen would go live in Gram's house until Gram got well enough to come home. Wouldn't Gram be surprised when she found them waiting for her? They would have to be careful, of course. They would have to stay away from any windows the neighbors could see into, and they couldn't use any lights at night, and they wouldn't be able to go outside, but there was plenty of food. Gram always kept her freezer and her cupboards well stocked, and they would be able to look out the kitchen window to watch the barges—if they wanted to watch barges. It would be like camping. It would be fun.

The problem was getting there. River Bluffs must be at least ten miles from the Becks' home, Renny figured, and it was a good fifteen from Prairieville, where they went to school. There were no buses that ran between the two towns, even if she and Karen had the money, which they didn't. They could hitchhike she supposed, but Gram had always warned her against hitchhiking. She would be afraid to do that. Besides, if whoever picked them up wasn't the kind to do something terrible to them, he would probably be the kind who would consider it his duty to turn them over to the police. Renny didn't know if they put kids as young as Karen in jail for running away, but she herself was only three years younger than Cynthia, and they had put Cynthia in jail. She figured she could walk the distance, but she didn't know about Karen. If she was going to take Karen, she would have to wait until the weather got a little better. If it was warm enough, they could sleep out in a field one night on their way to Gram's.

Spring came slowly. Friday, as they were walking home from the bus stop, thick, white flakes of snow began to fall, and Renny stamped her foot with frustration. Karen ran back and forth on the dirt road that led to the Becks' house, catching snowflakes on her tongue. Renny was cross with her when her boots splashed some mud. Karen said she was sorry, and she quit running. She took Renny's hand and walked quietly beside her, ignoring the snow. Renny apologized for being cross and twirled around in the middle of the road with her face up and her tongue out to catch the snowflakes, just to make Karen feel better.

But her heart wasn't in it, and Karen seemed to know.

Wait until they got to Gram's house. She would make everything up to Karen when they were at Gram's house. And when Gram came home, she would be glad to have Karen stay. Karen could become part of their little family. She wouldn't be any work for Gram, because Renny would take care of her.

Renny sat up in the middle of the night, not knowing what had awakened her. Was it time for church already? She had been dreaming about the church service, and Cynthia had been moaning, "Jesus, Jesus," or had she been the one doing the moaning? She shivered at the thought, and ducked back under the covers next to Karen. It was still dark. Sunday morning was hours away. She wished there were something she could do to keep from having to go to church with Pop Beck again, but she didn't know what it could be. She couldn't fake being sick and stay upstairs in bed, that was for sure. She was about to close her eyes and turn over to snuggle up against Karen when she saw a silhouette in the doorway. She sat up.

"Who's there?"

"Shhh." It was Cynthia.

"What are you doing with all your clothes on in the middle of the night?"

"I'm getting out of here," came the whispered response.

Renny swung her feet over the edge of the bed. "Where are you going?"

Cynthia moved toward Renny, and Renny could see she was carrying her cardboard suitcase. "Promise you won't tell nobody?"

"Of course I won't tell. What do you think I am?"

"I'm meeting Bill, by the water tower in Prairieville, at two A.M."

"Bill? Isn't he the one who's in jail, in the pen?"

"Yeah. But he was getting out today. He got time off for good behavior, and he's coming to get me. We're going to California. He's gonna marry me."

"Are you sure?" Renny asked, trying to imagine the crack in the cell wall through which this romance had flourished.

"Of course I'm sure. He said so. I've got his letter right here." Cynthia patted her pocket.

"How will you get to California?" Renny asked slowly.

"We'll hitch most likely. I've got some money, but we'll need that when we get there."

"Isn't that dangerous?"

"What?"

"Hitching?"

"Don't be silly. I'll have Bill with me."

Renny stopped for a moment to wonder whether traveling with a man just out of the penitentiary might not be more dangerous than hitching, but then she put that thought aside. "Cynthia, can I come with you?"

"To California? With me and Bill?"

"No, just to Prairieville, and then we can hitch to River Bluffs. I'm going to go back and live in my gram's house. I've got the key. You and Bill could hide out there for a few days until the police quit looking for you. They'll be looking for you, you know." Renny's mind was racing. It was about five miles into Prairieville. Karen could make five miles. She and Cynthia could take turns carrying her if they had to.

Cynthia sat down on the edge of her bed. "Well, I don't know. . . ."

"Please, Cynthia. We won't be any trouble. We're going to go soon anyway, but I'm afraid to hitch by myself."

"We? Who's we?"

"Me and Karen. Who else?"

Cynthia began to laugh softly. "You mean you plan to drag that little squirt along?"

Renny bristled. "Of course. I couldn't go off and leave her here, could I?"

"I don't know why not." Cynthia stood again and picked up her suitcase. "Look, kid, I've got to get moving. If you want to come, just you, I'll give you three minutes to get dressed and get your things. But I'm not dragging any thumb-sucking baby along."

Renny sat on the edge of the bed, looking at the dark figure that loomed over her and then back at the still lump in her bed that was Karen. The whole point of her plan was to get Karen out of here so she would be safe, wasn't it? She shook her head. "Forget it," she said.

Cynthia moved toward the door.

"Cynthia?"

"What?"

"I hope you and Bill make it to California okay. I mean, good luck and all that."

"Thanks."

Renny sat up in bed and listened for a long time after she had heard the front door shut softly.

In the morning, Renny sat rubbing her eyes against the thin light, looking at Cynthia's unmade bed. Empty. Of course it was empty. Cynthia was probably on her way to California with Bill by now.

"Where's Cynthia?" Karen asked, later, as Renny buttoned her dress.

Renny hesitated. Should she tell Karen? It probably didn't matter now. Cynthia and Bill would have had a good head start. They might be all the way across Missouri if they had been lucky with rides. "She's gone to meet her boyfriend," she said, "Bill, the one she met in jail. He's out and they're going to California. Don't say anything to anybody about it, though. We'll just pretend we don't know until Pop Beck finds out for himself, because he'll be mad."

To Renny's amazement, Karen turned around, threw her arms around Renny, and burst into tears. "Oh, Renny, don't," she sobbed. "Don't, don't!"

"Don't what?" Renny knelt and cupped the small, trembling chin in her hand. "Hey. What's wrong?"

"Don't ever go away to California with your boyfriend. Don't leave me."

Renny laughed and kissed one wet cheek and then

the other. "Look, pixie, I don't even have a boyfriend, and if I had one, I certainly wouldn't be going to California with him. And anyway, what makes you think I would leave *you?* Who would I sleep with?"

Karen drew in a long, wavering breath. "Who is Cynthia going to sleep with?"

Renny flushed and turned away to look for Karen's socks. "Herself, I guess."

"Why doesn't she sleep with her boyfriend?"

"Because you don't sleep with boyfriends unless you marry them, and then they're not boyfriends, they're husbands, and that's different," Renny said, sharply.

"Oh," Karen said.

"Where's Cynthia?" Mom Beck asked. She was standing at the stove frying bacon and eggs for Pop Beck. Cliff, the new boy, was slumped at the dining-room table over a bowl of corn flakes, which he was mashing with the back of his spoon instead of eating.

Renny threw a warning glance at Karen. "I don't know," she answered. "Isn't she downstairs already?"

Mom Beck shook her head and went on spooning hot bacon grease over the eggs so that they would be done exactly the way Pop Beck liked them. "If she don't hurry, she's gonna miss her breakfast."

Renny reached for two cereal bowls and handed one to Karen. She wondered what Cynthia and Bill were having for breakfast.

When it was time to leave for church, Pop Beck stood in the hall, looking particularly austere in his black Sunday suit, and called, "Cynthia. We are leaving. Come along . . . *now*." Renny and Karen exchanged glances.

"Cynthia," Pop Beck repeated, more sternly, "come down here immediately. We are ready to leave." Cliff turned his back on the group, which stood in a semicircle at the bottom of the stairs. Karen gazed up the stairs, as though she expected Cynthia to emerge at the sound of Pop Beck's voice.

"Mrs. Beck. Go get that girl," Pop Beck said sternly, and he planted his feet more firmly. Mom Beck took hold of the railing and started up the stairs, leaning forward and grunting slightly over each step. Everyone stood and waited. A fly made lazy circles over them. It had buzzed away toward the kitchen before Mom Beck emerged from the girls' room and started down the stairs, holding the railing and leading always with her left foot.

She didn't speak until she reached the bottom of the steps. "She's not there," she said. "Neither is any of her things. She must have gone in the night." She opened her mouth as if to say more, but watching Pop Beck's face, she closed it again.

Pop Beck turned and glared at Renny and Karen, as though they had hidden Cynthia. "Where is she?" he asked.

Karen shrank back against Renny's side. Renny said, "She went to bed the same time we did last night."

"But where is she?" He dropped his fierce gaze to Karen, who looked at the floor and squirmed.

"I don't know for sure," she said, but the words were very faint.

"Then where do you think she is, Karen?" Pop Beck's voice was gentler now, but no less demanding.

"I think," she said, in a tiny voice, "she went to California with Bill."

Pop Beck put his hand on Karen's shoulder. "And who is Bill?" he asked.

"Her boyfriend," she said, "the one she met in jail, but Renny said she's not going to sleep with him until they get married, so it's all right."

Pop Beck squared his shoulders and drew himself very tall. Renny was sure he was going to begin shouting, but instead he just said, very quietly, "Let us pray," and he knelt in their midst.

Everyone knelt around him, Mom Beck assisting herself down with the end of the banister, and Cliff sighing loudly behind them and thumping down.

"Lord of justice," Pop Beck began in a commanding voice, "Lord to whom all sinners may appeal, Lord who raised up the woman taken in adultery from the dust and commanded her to sin no more, forgive Cynthia her most terrible transgression; protect her from the consequences of her unspeakable sin, and may her error be an example to these young girls beside me that they may live in purity in order that they may come unblemished into Your most awful presence and that their souls may not be forever damned. Amen."

He stood up and brushed off the knees of his pants, though Renny didn't see any dust on them, and spoke to Mom Beck, who was struggling to her feet. "Go call the police. Give them a complete description of Cynthia. Tell them to hold her when they find her. We don't want her back here." He turned for the door. "Hurry," he called back, "or we'll be late for church."

Renny stepped with Karen's hand in hers out into the morning sunshine. The light was directly in her eyes and for a moment she couldn't see, and then she could see. Pop Beck was going to have Cynthia sent back to jail—and from there probably to the girls' reformatory. Renny's scalp prickled. Pop Beck, who talked about Jesus all the time but touched Renny with hands that made her feel sick all over, was angry with Cynthia because she had gone somewhere with a boy—a man—and he was going to throw her away, as he threw everybody away who didn't please him. Her knees felt like liquid and a great wave of nausea passed through her.

"I hate you," she said to Pop Beck's back.

Pop Beck, who was opening the car door, turned slowly and looked at Renny. "What did you say?" he asked. He was very calm.

"I said I hate you," Renny repeated, distinctly.

"What's this about?" He made no move toward her.

"You don't forgive anybody. Not for anything. Not Ralph. Not Cynthia. Well, I don't forgive you, either. And neither does God."

A hard smile covered Pop Beck's face, but he didn't respond. Mom Beck had come out onto the porch and was blinking in the sunlight. Karen was gripping

Renny's hand so hard that it hurt, but Renny let her hang on. Cliff was standing to one side, looking amused.

Renny stared at Pop Beck, who climbed carefully into the driver's seat, adjusting his Sunday suit as he sat down. Just before he pulled the door shut, he spoke to her, never raising his voice. "You may stay here, Lorraine. Go to your room. The rest of you get in. This is the Lord's day, and we are going to church." He slammed the car door.

Karen clung to Renny, and Renny, who was trembling now with the enormity of what she had done, gave her a gentle push.

"Go on," Renny whispered. "I'll be all right. I'll be here when you come back." The little girl moved reluctantly toward the car.

Renny stood on the porch for a long time after the car was gone, looking across the fields, still bare but black now with spring mud. She thought of Pop Beck and his careful black Sunday suit and his ice-blue eyes. She thought of her father, who wasn't really her father, who had never even existed, in spite of all her dreams and Gram's stories. She thought of Gram, alone in the hospital.

Finally she turned and went upstairs to her room.

11

THE door closed sharply. Footsteps on the stairs. Renny gasped and sat up in the middle of her bed. They must be home already. Pop Beck was coming up to talk to her. She scrambled off the bed and stood in the middle of the room. But where was there to go?

The door to the room opened, and Cynthia walked in.

"Cynthia," Renny gasped. "You came back!"

Cynthia dropped her battered suitcase and sat down on the edge of her bed. She looked grimy and tired, and her face was streaked with dust . . . and something more than dust. "He didn't come," she said to the floor.

"Oh." Renny sat down on the couch and stared at Cynthia, but she didn't move. Finally Renny added, "I'm sorry," but Cynthia still made no response.

"Maybe he was delayed," Renny said. "Maybe he's coming still. Maybe he'll call you when he gets to town."

Cynthia shook her head. "He never meant to come.

He was just playing tricks on me. He used to love playing tricks. He probably isn't even out of prison yet."

"Did you walk all the way to the Prairieville water tower and back?" Renny asked after a moment.

"I walked all the way there. I hitched most of the way back."

"Weren't you scared about hitching? Weren't you scared somebody'd try to do something to you?"

Cynthia looked at Renny and then back at the floor again without altering her expression. "It don't matter," she said. "By the way, how come you aren't in church?"

"Because Pop Beck told me to stay home."

"Since when?"

"I guess I was mad because he had Mom Beck call the police to get you. I told him I hated him."

Cynthia laughed. "You're some kid, you know?" Then she stood up and took some bills out of her jeans' pocket. "Did the old man miss the money?"

Renny jumped to her feet. "What money? You mean you took money from Pop Beck?"

"Yeah. I didn't think I'd ever be back here. Thought we would be out of the state by now, that it wouldn't matter. They don't give you much to start on when you get out of prison. I knew we would need money." Cynthia fingered the bills but without really looking at them.

"You'd better put that back," Renny said. "He had Mom Beck call the police. I don't know if he'll let you

111

stay or not, but I'm sure he doesn't know about the money, and he'd better not find out." Renny walked to the window and looked out, more tense now over Cynthia's plight than her own. She turned back to Cynthia. "How did you get it?"

"Saturday when I was cleaning Pop Beck's room I just cleaned out his dresser drawer for him, too."

"Please put it back," Renny pleaded.

Cynthia didn't move. She wasn't smiling any more. She was pale. "I don't care if he puts me out or not. He can do anything he likes. I'll get out of this hole some day anyway."

"Why did you come back then?"

Cynthia sat down again, holding the money out in front of her but still not really looking at it. "I don't know. I was tired, I guess. No place else to go. I wanted to lie down. Besides, I knew if the police picked me up I'd have to go back to that stinking jail, and then to Chillicothe, I guess."

Agitated, Renny walked over to Cynthia's side. "Well then, for heaven's sake put that money back before they come home or you'll go there anyway! If the money isn't gone, Pop Beck won't have anything on you."

Cynthia looked up at her and smiled wryly. "For heaven's sake, huh?"

Renny slumped with discouragement and exasperation and answered quietly, "For yours, Cynthia, for yours."

Cynthia looked at her a moment and then got up

and went down the steps, tiptoeing, as though someone else were already in the house with them.

When she came back up, Renny asked, "Do you want to go with Karen and me when we leave?"

"Where're you going?" Cynthia asked, lying back on her bed with a groan.

"To my gram's house, like I told you, in River Bluffs."

"And what will you do there?"

"Just hide and wait for my great-grandmother to get out of the hospital. I'm sure she'll be well soon, now."

Cynthia waggled her head back and forth slowly on her pillow. "No thanks, kid. I guess I'll just stick it out here. At least Bill knows where to find me." She turned over to face the wall and was asleep and snoring in a couple of minutes.

Pop Beck was adamant. Lorraine must go. Cynthia could stay. She had seen the error of her ways and returned to the fold. But Lorraine, Lorraine was a troublemaker, a malcontent. She had a bad influence on the other children, particularly on Karen.

Renny stood before her place at the dining-room table, and Pop Beck's words rose in her mind like some distantly remembered litany, but she didn't answer them. They didn't matter. She felt remote, removed from the Becks by an indescribable distance. When it was her turn to confess, the idea of responding stirred, but then it died again and she remained silent and watched the stern displeasure that passed across Pop

Beck's face, marked it, but hardly related it to herself. She was leaving. Sooner than Pop Beck thought, too. His anger wasn't important. She would take Karen with her. She would find a way.

Karen climbed into Renny's lap after dinner, and Renny rocked her mechanically. "Don't worry, little bird"—that was what Gram had often called her—"don't worry. It will be all right."

Karen shook her head without taking her thumb out of her mouth. "No, it won't. I won't stay here without you. I won't stay!"

"You won't have to," Renny whispered. "You and I are going away."

"Going away?" Karen sat up on Renny's lap and let her thumb drop. "Where are we going, Renny?"

"Shhh," Renny said. "We're going to go to my great-grandmother's house. We're going to wait there for her to come home. But it's a secret. You mustn't tell anybody. Not anybody at all."

"Can I tell my daddy?" Karen asked, beginning to glow with the pleasure of the secret. "Can I tell just him?"

"No, not even your daddy. But we'll go before you have time to see him again. Then after Gram comes home, he can come and visit you at Gram's. Will that be okay?"

Karen nodded. "Tell me about your gram, Renny. Is she nice? Does she like little girls?"

"My gram's very nice, and she loves little girls. She tells the most wonderful stories, all about. . . ." Renny hesitated, and then she stood up, putting Karen on the floor. "But first we have to make our plans, then I'll tell you about Gram."

Renny and Karen turned right when they got to the end of the Becks' lane, and kept walking.

"I wish I could bring my clown, just my clown," Karen whispered, though there was no one to hear them.

"I explained why you couldn't bring your clown. Mom Beck might have noticed, and she would know that you don't take your clown to school. Besides, your daddy will get it for you after my gram comes home from the hospital."

Karen put her hand in Renny's and skipped, once on each foot. She smiled up into Renny's face. "It's going to be fine, isn't it, Renny?"

"Of course it is," Renny reassured her, "and you'll have your clown again in no time." She was looking over her shoulder to make sure they were early enough to walk out of sight before the bus got to their lane. It would turn off on a side road a short way past the lane, but she didn't begin to breathe normally until she couldn't see their lane anymore or the road the bus would turn on. What would the driver do when he found no one there? Probably just go on. Renny couldn't imagine his waiting very long.

They each carried a sack lunch—Mom Beck had agreed to let Renny pack lunches for both girls because they complained of being tired of the cafeteria food—

and a few precious belongings of very small size were tucked away in their pockets and in their lunch bags. Renny carried her remaining half of the canasta deck under her sandwich.

They walked in the ditch between the road and the corn field so as to be less noticeable to cars, but the walking was uneven and, increasingly, the bottom of the ditch was muddy. Finally, they climbed to the side of the highway, crossed it, and began to walk along the side against the traffic.

"Everybody will know we aren't hitchhikers," Renny explained, "because we're on the wrong side of the road."

"Don't you want to be a hitchhiker?" Karen asked.

"No." Renny shook her head firmly. "Sometimes people in cars hurt people they pick up. So we'll just walk it. It's a long walk, but once we get to Gram's house we can fix a nice supper. How would you like some cocoa with supper?" *I hope, I hope*, she thought, *we can make it before night.*

"Nummm. I think I'm hungry now. Can I eat my sandwich?"

"How can you be hungry? You just finished breakfast!"

Karen grinned. "It would be more fun to eat it than carry it. My hand gets tired."

"Here. Let me carry your sack for a while. You can't get tired. We've just started. And you can't eat your lunch yet or you'll be starved before we get there."

Karen sighed, but she plodded along next to Renny in a good-natured way. Though the day was cool, the sun was shining brightly, and the light breeze promised spring. Renny wondered what they would have done if they had awakened to a Monday-morning rain. Go to school, she supposed, and wait for another day.

And what would Mom Beck do when they didn't get off the bus that night. She knew what Pop Beck would do when he came home for supper. Pray for them, of course. Then he would have Mom Beck call the police. Would Cynthia tell on them? No, Cynthia might not do much of anything for them, but she wouldn't tell on them.

Every time a car passed, Renny took Karen's hand and looked steadily ahead and walked a little faster. Although nobody slowed or seemed to notice them in any way, Renny knew she was taking a chance walking along the highway. Two kids by themselves were pretty conspicuous along the highway on a school day, but she was afraid of getting lost if they tried to cut across the fields. Besides, walking was harder in the fields.

"Renny?" Karen began to drag her feet and to pull back on Renny's arm after they had hurried past another car. "My side hurts."

Renny stopped and looked down at her companion.

"Bad," Karen added, looking up into her face and then down at the ground.

Renny tried to guess how far they had walked. Probably no more than a mile. "Okay," she said, try-

117

ing to sound cheerful, "time to take a rest. Can you walk as far as those trees up there so we can sit behind them?"

Karen looked at the large evergreen trees doubtfully, but she nodded her head.

After they had sat for a while, Karen said, "I feel better now. Should we eat our lunch?"

"No, not yet. It's not nearly lunchtime yet."

"Oh." Karen was obviously disappointed. "My tummy thinks it's lunchtime."

"Well, tell your tummy it's still morning. You should have eaten more breakfast."

"But my tummy didn't want any more breakfast then," Karen pouted. "It was too scared."

Renny laughed and hugged Karen. "Mine was scared, too, but we can't eat our food yet. Let's pretend we're crossing a desert and our lunches are water and we have to make every drop last or we'll die."

"Renny, I'm thirsty."

The girls stood up. "Real or pretend?"

"Real," Karen said. "What are we going to drink?"

Renny frowned. "I couldn't put anything to drink in our lunches because Mom Beck knows we can buy milk at school for three cents, so I have the money instead."

"Can we buy something then?" Karen said, as they began walking again.

"There's no place between here and River Bluffs to buy anything that I know of, and if we did find some place, even putting our money together, six cents won't buy much except at school."

"Will we die?" Karen asked softly.

"No, no. Of course not. We may get a little thirsty, that's all. I put an apple in for each of us and some celery. Those will help. And when we get to Gram's, I'll fix hot cocoa with marshmallows floating on top, lots of them."

"I'd rather have cold milk."

"Okay, a big glass of cold milk, then."

They walked in silence. Finally, Karen said, tentatively, "Renny, my feet just can't walk any more. Can we sit down?"

They sat, not looking for a tree this time. Some large, puffy clouds were scudding across the sky. When they covered the sun, both girls began to shiver. The ground was damp. Karen laid her head against Renny's shoulder. After a while Renny asked, gently, "Do you think your feet can walk now?"

Karen looked down at her brown school oxfords. They were muddy and scuffed. "They'll try," she said, and both girls got up and began walking again. Renny wondered if they had gone two miles yet. Perhaps three. There wasn't any way of keeping track. They were walking more slowly now. Much more slowly. Karen didn't let go of her hand any more.

"Renny?" This after they had been walking for a while. "Do you suppose it's lunchtime yet?"

Renny looked down at the little girl. Her feet were dragging. "I'm not sure what time it is," she said, "but I'm starved. What do you say we eat?"

Karen's face brightened.

"See those bushes up there alongside the fence?"

119

Renny pointed. "Let's have our lunch behind those."

Karen nodded and sighed. "Are you tired, Renny?" she asked as they plodded toward the bushes.

"Yes," Renny admitted, "I'm tired, but I will feel better after we eat."

Karen sighed again. "I will, too," she said.

They ate lunch sitting inside a pasture where black and white cows grazed some distance away.

Renny began to wish she had fixed something other than peanut butter and jelly. The peanut butter stuck to the roof of her mouth. She took out her milk money and shook it in her hand.

"Here," she said to Karen, who was scraping the roof of her mouth with a finger, "eat your apple. That will help."

It did help . . . a little.

When they began walking again, the clouds had piled up and filled the sky. The wind was sharper. Karen's teeth began to chatter.

"You get cold easier right after you eat," Renny said. "It's because your blood is working at digesting your food instead of warming you. Gram told me that. If we try to walk a little faster, we'll get warm."

Karen nodded, but she didn't walk any faster. "Tell me about your gram again, Renny," she said.

"Well," Renny began, "she has the most beautiful hair. Long . . . like your mother's, only she wears it in a braid wrapped around her head. I always do the braid for her. And there isn't a bit of gray in it. Not a bit. It's darker than your mother's, kind of a brown-red. And Gram's never cross. She likes little girls. And she's not really old, the way you would expect a great-grandmother to be. She always says, 'You're as young as you feel, and I feel like springtime.' She's like a friend and a mother and a grandmother all in one. And she tells stories. She makes the world seem like a nice place to be, even . . . ," Renny hesitated and looked down at Karen who was watching her expectantly, "even when it's not."

A slow smile erased the lines of fatigue from Karen's face. "I'm going to like Gram," she said.

12

RAIN was falling in a fine drizzle, so fine that at first there had seemed to be no wetness. Now Renny and Karen stood by the side of the road, their hair dripping, the shoulders of their jackets soaked through. Karen's teeth were chattering. The sky was too heavy with dull, gray clouds for the sun to show, and the afternoon was growing darker. Some of the cars that sped past them, throwing up another fine shower of wetness, already had their lights on.

"Where are we going?" Karen asked, as they hesitated at the edge of the road.

"We're going across to the other side so we can hitch a ride," Renny responded more firmly than she felt.

"But Renny, I thought you said. . . ."

"I know what I said, but it's getting late; you can't walk any farther, and we can't stop out here in this. Don't worry. I won't let anybody hurt you. Come on. Let's get across the road."

The girls scurried across the road and began walking slowly along the other side. When a car came by, Renny turned and looked at it expectantly, but it whished past as all the rest had done. Nobody seemed very worried about a couple of kids out on the road. Earlier she had been grateful for the lack of attention. Now she felt abandoned.

The next time a car came up from behind them, she held her thumb out tentatively, but still it didn't stop. She grew more bold as car after car zoomed past them and as Karen wilted beside her. Finally, a car slowed and pulled to a stop a short distance past them. Renny took Karen's hand and began to run toward the car, her heart pounding. What would they do if they got into a car with somebody and the person took them some place they didn't want to go and did something terrible to them? Maybe there were worse people in the world than Pop Beck.

As they came alongside the car, Renny slowed to a walk and said to Karen, "Just let me do the talking. If we tell them too much we might end up back at the Becks'." *Or in jail*, she added to herself mentally.

A grandfatherly-looking man leaned across the front seat and opened the door for them. "What are two little girls doing out in the middle of nowhere on a day like this?" he asked, but he didn't sound angry or upset.

"Please, sir," Renny said, "we've been visiting our cousins and their car broke down and we have to get back to our grandmother's house in River Bluffs." She squeezed Karen's hand more tightly as a reminder not to say anything.

"And they let you walk all the way back by yourselves? Why, we're near five miles from River Bluffs. What's wrong with those people? Get in, girls. Get in."

Renny hesitated by the open car door. He looked friendly. His hair, what he had of it, was white, and his scalp where there was no hair was pink and shiny, and his fingernails were cut square and clean. Gram always said you could tell a lot about a person by his fingernails.

"May we ride in the back, please?" she asked.

The man searched Renny's face as though he might be looking for something and nodded, gravely. Renny and Karen climbed into the back seat and pulled the door closed. They stayed huddled in the corner farthest from the driver. He leaned over and closed the front door; then they swung out onto the highway and were driving toward River Bluffs. The car was warm and music was playing on the radio.

Renny looked around the car covertly. Everything was clean and plush, a kind of silver green. Peering over the front seat she read a plaque on the dashboard. It said JESUS DIED FOR YOUR SINS. An involuntary gasp escaped her, and she drew back in the seat sharply.

"Is something wrong?" The man was watching her in the rear-view mirror. He looked concerned.

"No. I mean . . . well . . . why do you have that?" She pointed over the seat to the plaque which was imitation wood lettered in gold.

"This?" He ran his fingers across the deeply indented letters. "Because I believe it. Why do you ask?"

Renny was too exhilarated with relief and fatigue to think of any answer but the truth, though she had intended to be very careful not to reveal anything. "It's just that there was this man we were . . . with, and he believes like that."

The driver nodded. "You mean he is a Christian."

"Yeah." Her voice was heavy with contempt. "He's a *Christian*."

"You didn't like him?" he inquired.

"He's a terrible man," Renny said.

"So you're both going . . . home." It wasn't a question, but he made it sound like a question, especially when he said "home."

"Yes, sir." Renny's heart had begun to pound. She had said too much. He would know they were running away, and he would take them to the police, or he would do something bad to them. She edged closer to Karen, her arm around her, squeezing her. As soon as they got to River Bluffs, when they stopped for a light, she would open the door, and they would get out . . . before he could do anything.

"Where's home?"

"We live with my grandma, on High Street, the three-hundred block." They were getting near the town. Renny recognized a gas station and a garden shop.

"But the man you were with . . . ?"

"He talks about Jesus all the time."

They pulled up at a red light, but Renny didn't reach for the door. She was watching the driver's face in the mirror. He seemed to be about to say something.

They rode several blocks in silence, stopped at another stoplight, started again. Then the car pulled over to the curb and stopped short of a corner and Renny's heartbeat almost stopped her breath before she looked up to see that they were at Third and High Streets, just down from Gram's house, right where she had asked to go.

The driver turned in his seat to look directly at the girls. His eyebrows were bristly over eyes that were dark as shadows. "You will find Jesus," he said quietly, "in the hearts of those who profess Him. But not everyone who uses His name is a Christian. Is this where you wanted to go?"

Renny swallowed hard. "Yes, sir."

"Do you girls need anything? Are you in some kind of difficulty?"

Renny shook her head. She was reaching around Karen, fumbling for the door handle.

"Oh, no," Karen chimed in. "Renny's Gram likes little girls. She's going to take care of us as soon as. . . ."

"We get there," Renny finished hurriedly, opening the door and easing Karen out. "She'll be worrying about us if we don't hurry." She climbed out herself. "Thank you." She bent over to look back into the car before she closed the door. "Thank you very much."

The man smiled. She had been wrong. His eyes weren't dark. They had lights in them. "God be with you," he said.

Renny stood next to Karen and watched as the car pulled from the curb and turned on Bluff Street and moved silently away.

"Come on, Karen," she said, taking her hand. "Everything's all right, and we're almost there."

They began walking the last block to Gram's house. She already had her other hand inside her jacket, wrapped around the key.

The first indication Renny had that something was wrong was the sign in Gram's front yard. It was a realtor's sign that said FOR SALE in large red letters on a white background. Even Karen stopped and gazed at the sign.

"There must be some mistake," Renny said. "They've put the sign in front of the wrong house," and she pulled at the sign and wiggled it back and forth until she could pull it from the ground and drop it on its face on the pale, yellow grass. "Come on, Karen. Let's go in."

"Now we'll be . . . ," Renny said, as she swung the front door open, but she stopped. Gram's house—her house—was empty. Absolutely empty. The carpeting was still there and the drapes, but there wasn't a stick of furniture. Not Gram's rose velvet sofa or the walnut whatnot that held part of her china cup collection; not even Gram's rocker, the cane-backed rocker that had belonged to Gram's own mother and that squeaked so soothingly when anybody rocked in it. The pictures were gone from the walls and the vase of dried flowers and peacock feathers was no longer on

127

the mantel. There were no books in the glass-enclosed book cases set in the wall, and beyond the living room, Renny could glimpse the bareness of the dining room. Even the massive oak dining table was gone.

She leaned back on the door and it shut behind her with a click. "Oh, Karen," she said, "what have they done with my gram?"

Karen moved closer to Renny and took her hand in a protective gesture, but she said nothing.

The two girls began walking through the house, room after room. All empty. All bare. Renny stood for a moment at the kitchen window, watching the Mississippi rush and foam as it came through the dam, the river looking white and clean for a moment before it went back to its quiet mud brown. She turned away from the window and walked into the hall and into Gram's room. Her footsteps on the hardwood floors echoed off the bare walls. Gram's bed was gone, of course. Renny sat down, suddenly, in the middle of the floor and began to sob. Karen stood next to her patting her shoulders and stroking her hair.

They slept that night on the floor in Renny's room. Before they went to sleep, curled up together on the pale-blue shag carpet that had been Renny's choice when her room was redecorated, the girls sat for a long time watching the little yellow lights on the dam. The lights were repeated in the river. Renny had always liked the river lights better than the real ones that shone more steadily along the dam. Karen had complained only once of being hungry, and Renny had said that she was hungry, too, and then they had both gone to sleep.

The light streaming through the window awakened Renny first, and she got up carefully to keep from disturbing Karen, and tiptoed to the window. Every bone and muscle in her body ached, and her stomach was flat, caved in. The river hadn't changed. At least something remained the same. But then Gram always said that the river was different every minute. The same water never flowed past them twice. At least it looked the same, though. That was something.

"Dear God, please help me." Renny formed the words without sound, almost without thought. But whose god was she praying to? Not Pop Beck's. The god he talked about was hateful and a cheat. Pop Beck talked about love, but he meant something very different. She didn't think it could be Gram's god, either. Gram's god might be another kind of pretend, like her father coming home. And she didn't know anything about the god the man who had given them a ride spoke of. How could anybody know if there was a god anywhere, except in people's heads? How could anybody know anything?

Ralph didn't say there wasn't any God. He only said *he* didn't believe. He said he didn't believe in people, either, but he acted as if he believed in David, and in her. Maybe how you acted showed what you believed more than what you said. Well, it was time to act now. Karen had to have some breakfast.

When Renny turned away from the window, Karen was sitting up, rubbing her eyes and looking like a ruffled owlet.

"Hi," Renny said, "are you hungry?"

"I'm starved," Karen said. "Did you find some food?"

"No, but I know where we can get some."

"Where?"

"At my Great-Aunt Florence's. We'll have to walk again. It's about eight blocks from here . . . away from the river."

Karen jumped to her feet.

13

GREAT-Aunt Florence sat warming her hands on her coffee cup and watching the girls eat. The cup was one of Gram's collection of bone china.

"Why did you run away?" she asked for the third time.

Renny pushed her plate slightly to one side and pressed her napkin against her lips. "I was going to have to go soon anyway."

"I know. Then why couldn't you just wait for Miss Kistner to come and get you and not cause everybody all this worry? Do you know I spent half the night talking to Mr. Rawls? They contacted him when they knew you were both gone, and he came back from his business trip. He was almost beside himself."

Karen looked up from her plate with a smile at the mention of her father's name, but she went back to eating her scrambled eggs and toast and bacon without saying anything.

"I had to, Aunt Florence, don't you see? Once Miss Kistner had taken me some place else there would have been no one to look after Karen. I had to leave while I could still take her with me."

Great-Aunt Florence lifted her coffee to her lips but put the cup down without tasting it. "No, Lorraine, I don't see. I don't see anything, except that you are a willful, inconsiderate girl. Who took care of Karen before you got there?"

Renny squirmed in her chair. "No one was looking after her. Not properly."

"And you know what is proper and what isn't?"

"I know some of it, anyway. Gram taught me. And the Becks' isn't a good place for Karen. I know that."

"Then what is a good place?" Great-Aunt Florence demanded. Her face was bunched up like a prune and there were dark smudges under her eyes. "Hiding away in your great-grandmother's house?"

"It's my house, too!"

"Yes, and once it was my house. You seem to think you're the only one who ever lived there."

"I know you and my grandpa grew up there. Only *you* moved away to your own apartment. Left Gram alone. If it hadn't been for my mother, and then me, she wouldn't have had anybody after Grandpa John died."

Great-Aunt Florence pushed her cup away sharply and the coffee slopped into the saucer. "Yes, my brother John stayed around for a while, brought his daughter home for Mother to take care of when his wife died, as if Mother hadn't earned a rest. And then your mother left and came back with you. Now, when your great-grandmother is sick you come back with this child, as though it can go on forever. Well, it can't. There is an end to some things, Lorraine."

Renny stood up, shoving her chair back roughly, and leaned on the table that separated her from her great-aunt. "I'm taking care of Karen. I wasn't going to ask Gram to do it. And I'm going to take care of Gram, too. I wouldn't put her in the hospital with a bunch of strangers. I'm going to bring her home and take care of her."

Great-Aunt Florence picked up a paper napkin and folded it carefully into quarters and put it under her cup to soak up the spilled coffee. "You're going to take care of everybody, aren't you? Just like my mother."

"At least I'll try. That's more than you do."

Great-Aunt Florence looked up slowly, and to Renny's amazement she smiled, but there was nothing happy in the smile. "A person can pay a great price for 'taking care of' or for being taken care of."

"What do you mean?" Renny sank back to her chair.

"Just that." Great-Aunt Florence stood up and carried her cup to the kitchen, her mouth clamped shut in a tight line.

Renny looked at Karen and shrugged. Karen shrugged back. Renny gathered up her dishes and headed for the kitchen where Great-Aunt Florence stood over a sink of steaming dishwater. Renny hesitated, her plate in her hand.

"I'll take care of it, Lorraine. Just put it down."

Renny set her dishes on the counter and went back

for Karen's. After she brought those in and set them down, she stood back and folded her arms across her chest.

"How is Gram, Aunt Florence?"

At first Renny didn't think Great-Aunt Florence was going to answer—she was bent over the few dishes so intently—but finally she said, "There hasn't been any change."

"What does that mean?" Renny could feel her chest tighten and her breathing becoming more difficult.

"It means," she said sharply, "that you saw her on the morning she had her stroke, and that's how she is."

"But she's in the hospital. They're taking good care of her. She must be getting better."

Great-Aunt Florence dried a china cup with great care and set it in her cupboard. Renny could see other cups of Gram's near where she set it. "She's not in the hospital any more," she said, finally.

"She's not . . . but where is she then? What have you done with her?"

Aunt Florence released the plug in the sink and the soapy water swirled down the drain. "I haven't done anything with her," she said, still bent over the sink. "There was nothing more they could do in the hospital. She's in a nursing home."

"A nursing home?" Renny almost shouted. She wanted to grab Great-Aunt Florence by the arm and make her turn around. "You put my gram in a nursing home?"

Aunt Florence turned slowly, her hands still glistening with water and soap suds. "Yes," she said, "I put *my mother* into a nursing home."

"Why? People get well in hospitals! They go to nursing homes to die."

Great-Aunt Florence stood, her hands dripping, unheeded, and her face softened. "That's right, Lorraine," she said, very quietly. "And that's what she's doing, in as much comfort and with as much care as we can give her."

"No!" Renny could feel the tears on her cheeks. "That's not true. I'm going to go get her. I'm going to bring her home. I'll take care of her. If I take care of her she won't die. I know she won't."

"Lorraine." Great-Aunt Florence put her hands on Renny's shoulders and Renny drew back, shaking herself free.

"She never mattered to you," she cried, the tears almost choking her. "You went off and left her. You never even cared!"

Great-Aunt Florence squared her shoulders and drew in her stomach. Her bosom quivered. "Eight blocks," she said, in a voice so quiet it was almost a whisper, but one Renny couldn't miss hearing. "I moved eight whole blocks to live alone in this apartment and take an office job I never wanted. I gave up college—I could have had a scholarship—because that would have taken me away from River Bluffs, away from Mother. I turned down a couple of men, too, though I imagine that's hard for you to believe."

"Why? Why did you?" Renny didn't care what

Great-Aunt Florence said. She, Renny, had been with Gram. Nobody else.

"Because I was taking care of her. For nearly forty years, Lorraine."

"But you never have. You've never taken care of her at all!"

"Who do you suppose paid for the new roof on the house last year or the paint job? Who do you suppose has paid for most of everything you have ever eaten or worn?"

"Not you!" Renny could feel her hands clenching into fists. "It couldn't have been you."

Great-Aunt Florence looked at Renny steadily, but she didn't say anything. Renny cast about in her mind for the familiar anger that had always kept a distance between her and Gram's daughter. It was easy enough to remember.

"You called my mother a slut once. I heard you. You never wanted Gram to keep me."

"You're right, I didn't. For her sake and for yours, too. And maybe a little for mine. She was all I had, only I never had her. First there was my brother, then Shelley, then you. Somebody always came first."

The doorbell rang, and Great-Aunt Florence left to go answer it. Renny leaned against the sink. She felt sick.

Mr. Rawls and Great-Aunt Florence sat across the living room from Renny and Karen. Mr. Rawls was rubbing his hands over his face, as though everything would look different when he quit rubbing. When he looked up at Karen and then at Renny he seemed resigned to nothing having changed.

"Okay, girls," he said, "you win. I still don't know what's wrong, but I will take it for granted that something is seriously wrong. Your aunt says you have always been a pretty reliable girl, Renny."

Renny looked at Great-Aunt Florence in surprise. Great-Aunt Florence was studying her folded hands.

"I'm going to change my job, Karen. Get one where I don't have to travel. I kept thinking it would just take a little more time, but your mother was right. It's been too much time now. I'm sorry I didn't do it in the beginning."

Karen watched her father with unblinking eyes, waiting to understand what he meant. Her hand had crept over and curled inside Renny's.

"As soon as I have the new job, you can come home."

Karen squealed and ran and threw herself into her father's arms. Renny's throat tightened. Karen was going to go home. Wasn't that what she had wanted, what she had been working for? The muscles in her throat ached and her face felt stiff.

Karen looked up from hugging her father, looked over at Renny, and her expression changed. "But what about Renny?" she asked, turning back to her father. "Where will she go?"

Mr. Rawls looked across at Renny and down at Karen. "I'm not sure," he said.

"Daddy? Can Renny come live with us? Can she, please? She wouldn't be any trouble, really. And she takes good care of me."

"But who would take care of her?" Mr. Rawls asked, kissing Karen's hair.

"You would, Daddy, and Mommy when she comes home."

Mr. Rawls looked across at Renny again, speculatively, then he turned to Great-Aunt Florence. "Where do you suppose Renny will be sent, Miss Morrison, since Mr. Beck has said he won't have her back?"

"Mr. Beck had asked to have her removed before the girls ran away," Great-Aunt Florence said. "Miss Kistner told me it's difficult to find foster homes for older children. She doesn't seem to have any place at the moment. I would let Lorraine stay with me for a time, but she has been too much with old people and with women. I don't want Miss Kistner to begin to think she has no responsibility to the child."

Renny squirmed on Aunt Florence's slick horsehair sofa. "Never mind," she started to say, "I'm going back with. . . ."

"Oh, please, Daddy, please!" Karen implored. "Renny wouldn't be any trouble. I know she wouldn't. She's my big sister."

Mr. Rawls spoke slowly, his eyes moving from Renny to Karen and back to Renny again. "I would have to talk to Miss Kistner . . . and your mother, of course, but perhaps if I will be home more. . . . How would you feel about that, Renny?"

"I wouldn't mind," Renny said with a slight shrug. The Rawls lived in River Bluffs. She could visit Gram at the nursing home. She could make plans for bringing her home.

"Then she can!" Karen broke away from her father and twirled across the room in crazy, laughing circles until she landed on top of Renny, limp and giggling.

"Wait a minute, Karen," Renny said, patting her bottom gently, "nobody has said that yet."

Mr. Rawls stood up. "One step at a time. First I'll talk to my boss; then I'll tackle Miss Kistner. I'll be back with a report this afternoon."

Miss Kistner was shocked, appalled at the idea of placing Renny in a home without a mother, but in the end she agreed, with a great show of reluctance, to a temporary placement. She had, for the moment, no better solution. Mr. Rawls' boss agreed to his shifting back to a department that didn't require traveling, with a cut in pay, and the girls stayed with Great-Aunt Florence while Mr. Rawls got everything ready for their arrival.

Renny avoided talking with Aunt Florence as much as possible. She didn't want to hear anything Aunt Florence had to say about Gram's illness. Aunt Florence was wrong. She had to be wrong. Gram had always told Renny that she would live to see her grown. She had promised.

Renny was shocked when Aunt Florence said she went only once a week to visit Gram, and that "for the

139

sake of the nurses." She said Gram didn't even know she was there.

"Gram will know I'm there," Renny replied, and Great-Aunt Florence just looked at her.

"It's time you let go," she said.

"You're jealous," Renny answered. "You told me so yourself."

Aunt Florence smiled a hard little smile. "You and I seem to bring out the worst in one another, Lorraine. We always have."

"That's not my fault!"

"No," Great-Aunt Florence smoothed down her dress, "I don't suppose it is. You didn't choose to be born to your mother when she was little more than a girl. You didn't choose to be brought up by an old woman."

"But I would have," Renny said quickly. "I would have chosen Gram if I could have had any family in the world."

Aunt Florence sighed. "She did to you what she did to me. It's too bad. We should have been friends. Perhaps I could have made it different for you."

Renny was blind with anger. Aunt Florence was trying to take away everything. Well, she wasn't going to have Gram. She wasn't going to say anything about her.

"I know exactly what Gram did to you. She took care of you. She was left all alone with you and Grandpa John when her husband was killed in the war, in World War I. And she took in laundry and sewing so you could survive because all she got was a little pension. I know. She told me."

Aunt Florence was very calm. "You're absolutely right, Lorraine. She took care of us, my brother and me. She even sat up at night and sewed . . . in the hall right outside our bedroom doors. She said the light was better there, but it wasn't, really. I would wake up and see her."

"What was wrong with Gram sewing in the hall?"

"The same thing that's wrong with her taking the place of your friends. Finally, there isn't anybody else, and then you owe her too much."

"She never made me think I owed her anything."

Great-Aunt Florence shook her head slowly. "Except your life, Lorraine. Nothing except your life."

Renny turned on her heel. She slammed the door as she went out to check on Karen, who was playing outside, waiting for her father to come. *I wouldn't mind owing Gram my life*, she thought, *if I could make her well.*

14

RENNY sat in the car for a few moments after Karen and her father had gone into the house. She pretended to be looking for something she had dropped. She looked so intently, in fact, that when she finally climbed out of the car and headed for the house, she was filled with the dismay of something lost.

She stopped in the doorway, surprised. Mrs. Rawls was there, looking flushed and pretty, and Karen was leaning against her, rubbing the hem of her mother's blouse between her fingers and thumb, as though it were part of a security blanket. Mrs. Rawls noticed her first.

"I'm back," she said, smiling at Renny. "I've come home."

"Oh," Renny said, not knowing anything else to say.

"Come and see your room, Renny," Mr. Rawls said. "It's all ready for you."

Renny followed Mr. Rawls and Karen into the hallway. Mrs. Rawls came along behind them all. Mr. Rawls stopped halfway down the hall and opened a door and stood back. Karen went in, but Renny stood in the hall, not moving.

The walls weren't blue, as her room had been at Gram's; they were painted the pale yellow of early-morning sunshine. But it was her room, filled with all her things. Everything she had left behind. Her own white and gold bed with the bookcase headboard and her dresser and the dressing table with the spindly legs and the little mirror. Everything she and Gram had picked out for her room when she was about Karen's age. And on its wobbly brown table in the corner was her record player and her albums. Even her bedspread and the old fuzzy stuffed dog she always kept on her bed.

"I painted this room last year." Mrs. Rawls was standing behind Renny, and she spoke very quietly, hesitating before she continued, "but we can repaint it if there is some color you like better."

Renny shook her head. "I like yellow, but how . . . where . . . that's my furniture, my things."

"Yes," Mr. Rawls said. "Your Aunt Florence had it stored for you. She and I thought it would be a nice surprise for you just to find it here, so we didn't tell you. We had it brought over as soon as we got the final word from Miss Kistner."

Renny leaned against the doorjamb. "But my things . . . they're supposed to be in Gram's house . . . waiting. You make it seem like I'm going to stay here, and I'm not. Didn't you know I wasn't?"

Karen, who had been standing in the middle of the

room, turning slowly and looking without touching a thing, ran to Renny and threw her arms around her waist. "But you are going to stay, Renny. You know you are."

"You saw that your great-grandmother's house is being sold," Mr. Rawls said.

"We slept in your room," Karen added, urgently, "and there wasn't anything in it at all."

"But where will Gram and I go when I get her from the nursing home?"

Mr. Rawls stood for a moment with his arms limp at his sides, looking helpless, then he stepped forward and put his arms around Renny. "We'll see what . . . ," he started to say, but Renny pulled away from him violently.

"Don't you touch me," she said. "Don't you ever touch me!"

Mr. Rawls backed off, his face registering bewilderment.

Renny spent the afternoon rearranging her clothes in her suitcases—Mr. Rawls had gotten her things from the Becks—but she didn't put anything away. She wasn't going to stay long enough to put anything away.

Mr. Rawls fried chicken for supper, and Mrs. Rawls made salad and mashed potatoes and gravy.

"Mmmm," Karen said, scooting into her chair while Renny still hesitated behind hers, "Daddy's chicken. My daddy makes the best chicken," she added, smiling across the table at Renny, a drumstick from the platter already in her hand.

"What's this?" Mr. Rawls exclaimed, sitting down at the head of the table. "No grace? We'll all get indigestion if the food isn't blessed."

Karen laughed and put her drumstick down. Mr. Rawls held out a hand to each side of the table, and Mrs. Rawls did the same. Karen immediately reached out to both of her parents. Renny sat and stared at the hands reaching across the table to her.

"Make a circle, Renny," Karen said. "We always make a circle."

Renny took Mrs. Rawls' hand and gave her other, limply, to Mr. Rawls.

"That way," Mr. Rawls said, "we know that nobody is snitching during the praying. All hands are accounted for and we all get an even start."

Renny didn't laugh with the rest of them. They could pray any way they liked, or not pray—it didn't matter to her. She would be home with Gram soon. They always sat for grace with their hands folded in their laps.

The rest of them talked as they ate. They had so much to tell one another. Karen told about walking from the Becks' to River Bluffs, about the teacher she had in Prairieville, about the game she had played with her friend Dawn that afternoon. Mr. Rawls explained that his boss had suggested he take a couple of courses in business management, so he could work toward a better position without having to travel. Mrs. Rawls told a story about a new woman who had come onto her ward just before she left who kept saying, "But you're crazy. You're all crazy," any time anyone tried to talk to her, and would go off into a corner and talk to herself to keep from having to talk with the "crazy people." Everyone laughed, except Renny, who was working at her drumstick awkwardly with a knife and fork the way Gram had taught her to.

"Karen," she said, when there was a break in the conversation, "it isn't polite to pick your chicken up in your hands."

Karen looked at her greasy hands and then at her parents in turn.

"It's all right, Renny," Mrs. Rawls said. "Fingers are allowed for chicken in this house."

"As long as they aren't wiped on the tablecloth or the wall," Mr. Rawls added.

Karen grinned and went back to eating her chicken. Renny flushed and kept working with her fork and knife.

"Tomorrow's Saturday," Mr. Rawls said, turning to Renny. "Two more days before you go back to school. What would you like to do?"

"I want to go visit my great-grandmother," Renny said quickly.

Mr. Rawls nodded, and he and Mrs. Rawls exchanged glances, which Renny saw but chose to ignore.

"All right," Mrs. Rawls said. "Perhaps Karen can play with Dawn in the morning, and Mr. Rawls and I can take you to the nursing home."

Renny nodded and smiled at Mrs. Rawls. She set down her knife and fork and picked up the drumstick.

In the morning Renny hurried through breakfast. Mrs. Rawls had made waffles, and Renny ate them, but she barely tasted anything. She had cleared the table and started washing dishes before anyone else had moved.

"Slow down, Renny," Mr. Rawls said. "Visiting hours don't begin until ten."

Renny didn't say anything, but she washed the dishes very slowly, declining anyone's assistance, and dried and put them away one dish at a time. She was going to see Gram. She didn't tell the Rawls that she was planning on bringing Gram home. She would talk to Gram about that; then Gram would tell them. They would have to listen to her. Even Great-Aunt Florence would have to listen to Gram.

In the car, riding in the front seat between Mr. and Mrs. Rawls, Renny could feel her heart pounding. Mrs. Rawls was sitting, twisting her hands in her lap. After a moment she looked down at her hands and stopped. Renny stared straight ahead. No one tried to talk.

When they pulled up in front of the nursing home, everyone sat in the car without moving for a moment. It was a huge old mansion that once had been a private home. Renny didn't think Gram would have liked to live in it even when it had been new. She was sure Gram wouldn't like it now.

The door opened into a lobby where men and

women with sunken faces sat around on couches and in wheelchairs, some sagging forward, staring silently at the floor. They looked fragile, their skin like the paper on the Chinese lantern Gram had given her when she was little. The room was filled with a musty smell, a decaying kind of smell mixed with other things, wax and disinfectant and the sharpness of urine. Gram didn't belong here. Renny was going to take her away today.

"Hello, little girl." A hand like a curved claw grasped Renny's arm. Renny turned toward the voice, steeling herself to keep from drawing away. The woman had no teeth. Her nose jutted out and her chin poked out and her mouth was a sunken black hole between them. Gram was never like that. She would never be like that. "It's nice to have a little girl here," the woman said.

Renny smiled weakly at the old woman and moved past her slowly, letting the hand fall away from her arm. All the eyes in the room followed her. On the other side of the lobby a tiny woman with the round face of a cherub was tied into a wheelchair. She looked up at Renny and her face creased into a smile. "Mama?" she said. Renny stood rooted where she was, in front of the woman with the upturned, questioning face.

"No," she said, gently. "I'm not your mama."

The woman's face crumpled, and for a moment Renny thought she was going to cry, but she caught sight of Mrs. Rawls coming behind Renny and repeated, with the same hopeful smile, "Mama?"

Mrs. Rawls didn't say anything, but she smiled back and put her hand on the woman's arm.

"My mama," the woman said, in a baby singsong, and she patted Mrs. Rawls' hand with a clumsy tenderness. She was still smiling when they all moved past her toward the nurse's station.

Mr. Rawls took charge. "This is Lorraine Morrison. She is here to see her great-grandmother."

The woman behind the desk signaled for a nurse's aide who motioned for them to follow her down a linoleumed hall and up a wide flight of stairs. "The ambulatory patients," she explained, "and those in wheelchairs are kept on the main floor so they can go to the dining room. Those who are bedridden are on the second floor."

Renny didn't listen to her. Her own pulse filled her ears. The doors they passed were open, but Renny didn't glance into any of them. She had seen all she cared to see.

Near the end of the hall, the woman stopped in front of a door and stepped back for Renny to go in ahead of her. Renny held her breath and kept her eyes on the floor as she walked in. She knew how surprised Gram would be. What would they say to one another? Panic seized her. She hadn't even thought of what she should say.

When she got to the bed she looked up and stopped so quickly that the aide, who had followed her in, stepped on her heel. In the bed was another fragile old woman with short white hair and a vacant, staring face. The woman's mouth hung open. A tube ran from

149

a bottle suspended by the bed to somewhere under the stiff white sheet. Furious, Renny turned on the aide.

"That's not my gram. I want to see my gram!"

The aide raised her eyebrows, which were plucked to a fine line, and turned to the Rawls. "Mrs. Morrison?" she asked. "Didn't you want to see Mrs. Morrison?"

Mr. Rawls nodded.

The nurse turned back to Renny. "That's your grandma, dear. Of course she won't know you. She doesn't know anybody. She's been just like that since she came."

Renny turned back to the bed. Was it? Could it be? Impossible. "Her hair," she said, "her beautiful hair. What have you done with it?"

The aide looked disconcerted for a moment. "Oh," she said, "oh, yes, I remember. She used to have long hair. We cut it not long after her daughter brought her here. It wasn't any use to her, just hurt her when you brushed it, and it was such a job to take care of. You've no idea what a job!"

"It wasn't a job," Renny said fiercely. "I brushed out her hair a thousand times. It was never a job."

The aide began checking the bottle, regulating the slow drip of the fluid which moved down the tube to the still form. "But with her lying there all the time, it just got mussed. And her daughter suggested we cut it," she explained reasonably.

"But the color," Renny said, refusing still to believe, "the color, it used to be. . . ."

"Kind of dark red, wasn't it? That was just a rinse, you know. When we washed it, it all came out."

"It couldn't have been. She never had a bit of gray in her hair . . . not ever. I know."

The aide studied Renny. "Nothing wrong with rinses, you know." She looked at the figure in the bed speculatively and back at Renny. "I suppose it's kind of a shock if you haven't seen her for a while. But we're taking good care of her. She's not suffering, not like it is with some of them who get so sad and confused. It can be a blessing, the way she is."

"Go away," Renny said, without looking at the aide. "Please go away."

"She hasn't seen her since the illness," Mr. Rawls explained in the background. "She needs some time."

Renny could hear the aide's cushioned step moving down the hall away from them. She stood perfectly still and stared at the woman they said was her great-grandmother. The cloudy blue eyes hardly blinked. They were utterly blank, like windows into an empty room.

"Gram," she said, moving up against the bed and lifting the pale hand that lay on top of the sheet. "Gram, it's me, Renny."

The hand that lay in Renny's was interlaced with knobby purple veins and freckled with brown age spots, but the fingers were narrow and tapering, delicately curved.

"Gram." Renny stroked the skin gently; soft it was, and as thin as a baby's. "I've missed you, Gram. I've come to get you, to take you home."

The old woman in the bed did not stir. The sheet rose and fell gently, as though stirred by a faint but persistent wind. Renny could feel every bone in the hand between her own.

"Are you tired, Gram, just a little? You can rest a while, and then we'll go."

Renny could sense Mr. Rawls moving toward her. She glanced up to see Mrs. Rawls putting a restraining hand on his arm.

"I'll talk to you for a bit, Gram. Would you like that? I know you're tired. You don't even have to answer. I'll talk and you listen, and then I'll help you get dressed and we'll go home."

Renny squeezed the hand carefully, but there was no answering pressure. She drew a deep breath and began, her eyes never moving from the familiar hand. Her words tumbled over one another. "It's been three weeks since I've seen you. Three whole weeks. Aunt Florence wouldn't let me stay at the house. She . . . she thought I needed a family, so she sent me to a foster home. There were lots of other kids there. There was Cynthia. Did you know they put kids in jail just for running away? And there was Ralph and David. I liked Ralph. You would have liked him, too, Gram. And then there was Karen. She's just like a little sister. I never had a little sister before."

Renny stopped and traced a swollen vein with one finger; then she covered them all. A pale, delicately freckled hand lay on the other side of the sheet. Renny gazed at it, and she went on talking.

"There was another boy before we left, but I didn't get to know him. His name was Cliff."

The hand Renny was watching moved up to smooth the pillow. Mrs. Rawls was bending over Gram slightly, watching her face with such tenderness that Renny kept her eyes on her, on her finely chiseled nose and her lips, softly parted.

"Our foster parents were Mom and Pop Beck. Mom Beck was okay. She meant well, like Ralph said. But Pop Beck . . . it was different with Pop Beck. He talked about Jesus all the time . . . and about sin. Mostly about sin. And one time, Gram," Renny was looking straight into Mrs. Rawls' eyes now, "one time he held me on his lap, and he touched me. He touched me all over, Gram, but I didn't want him to. Even if it felt good . . . I didn't want . . . him. . . ."

Renny's voice ran out, and she was left staring at Mrs. Rawls, who reached across and covered Renny's hand, Renny's hand and Gram's, with her own.

"I really didn't," Renny said in a faint whisper.

"And so you ran away," Mrs. Rawls finished for her. "You took Karen to keep her safe, and you ran away."

Renny nodded. "I was coming back to Gram," she said. "I wanted everything . . . everything to be like it was before."

There were tears in Mrs. Rawls' eyes that brimmed and clung to her pale lashes. "But sometimes we can't go back," she said.

Renny studied Mrs. Rawls' face for a moment, and

then she looked down at Gram for the first time, really looked at her. Her mouth was slack. A bit of spittle was on her cheek. Her face had lost form, meaning, character. Renny picked up a tissue from the bedside table and wiped Gram's cheek; then she put the tissue down and brushed the fine fluff of white hair away from her forehead. The eyes didn't reflect even the shadow of Renny's hand. She could almost feel the skull beneath the skin. She bent over and kissed Gram's forehead, softly.

"Gram," she said, "it's me, Renny. Wake up." There was no break in the pattern of steady breathing, no change in the quietness of the waxen face.

Renny straightened up. "She always loved me," she said. "Always."

"We know." Mr. Rawls had stepped close to Renny's side. "It shows."

"When I first went into her room that morning . . . with her tea . . . when I first saw . . . I couldn't believe. Gram was . . . everything." Renny looked across at Mrs. Rawls, up at Mr. Rawls, who was practically touching her. "Just everything."

"We're here, Renny." Mrs. Rawls' voice was firm and strong.

Renny nodded. She looked down at the placid face, withdrawn into some world where she could not reach, and she remembered what Gram had said to her every night for as long as she could remember.

"Sleep . . . sleep in peace," Renny whispered.

She stood for a long time, just watching Gram.

Then she turned to Mr. Rawls, who put his arm around her, letting her lean with her head against the hollow between his chest and shoulder. Mrs. Rawls joined them at the door, and together they walked down the corridor.